LETHAL OUTBREAK

LISA HARRIS

LYNNE GENTRY

AN AGENTS OF MERCY THRILLER

LETHAL
OUTBREAK

BEST-SELLING AUTHOR

LISA HARRIS
LYNNE GENTRY

For those who daily risk their lives on the medical frontlines. . .thank you.

ONE

Aiden Ballinger stepped outside the makeshift laboratory and felt the frigid winter air slip its icy fingers through the fabric of his heavy coat. He'd found every movement at the high altitude exhausting, but he'd also found a sense of tranquility he hadn't expected in the frozen tundra's barren landscape. The *roof of the world* was a fitting description for the Tibetan Plateau, standing over three miles above sea level and surrounded by the spectacular peaks of the Himalayan mountain range. But the very thing that mesmerized him, also terrified him.

Because this find was different.

He sucked in a breath and felt his lungs burn. He'd checked the results from the field testing a dozen times, then checked them again. It wasn't the first time an unknown bacteria or virus had been discovered in frozen tundra. Outbreaks like the one his Rapid Response Team had come to investigate were becoming more and more common. Industrial expansion across the globe was excavating viruses that had been buried for centuries as well as destroying the natural habitats of animals. With the ease and increase in international travel opportunities, it wouldn't take much to turn a small, localized outbreak into a worldwide pandemic. His job was to isolate and eliminate deadly pathogens before that happened. But this time, he hadn't been quick enough. His team had evidence, in the form of some very sick villagers, that the genetic signature of the recently uncovered virus was dangerous to humans right out of the gate. And that had him more than worried.

Aiden's SAT phone buzzed, and he took the call from his boss, hoping for better reception than last time. "Shepherd?"

"Aiden. . .sorry it took me so long to get through. Tell me what you've got."

"I sent you an encrypted email with the test results from the virus, but we need to move fast on this. We've recorded at least thirty-five newly infected people in the nearby village in the past forty-eight hours, and it's not slowing down."

"So the results are conclusive?"

"Conclusive enough that we need to do further testing in the States. We've been able to do an initial match between the virus we retrieved and those infected. Once verified, we'll be able to better respond."

"Agreed. I'm working on getting you out of there as soon as possible."

Aiden hesitated for a moment. "I'll be honest, I've never seen anything quite like this. We're looking at a viable giant virus with the potential—as already seen—to spread rapidly—"

"We need. . .exposed. . .spell disaster. . ."

"Shepherd. . ." Aiden tried moving up a slight incline, searching for better reception. "Shepherd, you're breaking up."

"Check. . .get packed. . .I'll arrange. . ."

Aiden hung up the call, frustrated. But cell reception was the least of his problems right now. They had yet to attempt to revive any of the pathogens they'd found, even though that didn't matter at this point. Not when they had evidence pointing to the fact that the virus had already found viable host cells in humans.

Calum "Iceman" Lewis stepped out of the Quonset hut designed for arctic conditions, then pulled his hood tighter around his face. "What are you doing out here, man? It's freezing."

"Trying to get a better signal. Trying to clear my head." Aiden walked back to his long-time friend and caught his gaze. "You looked at the last round of test results?"

"I did, but it's still inconclusive. We need to study the DNA's degradation—"

"If the virus's DNA wasn't viable, there wouldn't be an outbreak."

"Agreed, but I still think you're jumping to conclusions."

Aiden shook his head. "I might not be able to conclusively prove what we've found, but we both know that if there's going to be a viral outbreak on a grand scale, it's going to come from this exact scenario. These giant viruses have proven they can survive for long periods of time in harsh conditions. And we have evidence that it can infect humans."

Scientists had been warning about the situation for years. Ancient bacteria, viruses, and infectious microorganisms thawing and being released. Some believed there was little threat to humans because most of these pathogens couldn't survive indefinitely in harsh conditions or without a host. But in nature, there were always exceptions. Ebola was the perfect example of a virus that went into hiding only to emerge somewhere else unexpectedly. Up until now, there had never been any clear indication of where it had been or where it would show up again. But Ebola, like every virus, needed a place to hide between deadly outbreaks. Both bats and primates had been thought to be the place it chose, but there were still as many questions as answers.

"What do you want us to do?" Iceman's question broke through his thoughts.

"I'm going to head back to the States with samples of the virus while you finish up here. I want to have our initial findings retested in a high-security biolab in the US. We need to know exactly what we're dealing with."

"Okay."

"And Iceman. . ." Aiden turned and caught his friend's gaze. "We can't talk about this. To anyone. At least not until we can unequivocally verify the connection. News of the discovery of a prehistoric giant virus that has already infected humans *and* is spreading rapidly will only cause panic. Shepherd is working with the local government to ensure measures are put into place to slow the outbreak, but we need to tread carefully. And quickly."

"Agreed, but maybe *you* need to slow down." His friend reached out and squeezed Aiden's shoulder. "I can tell that your mind has already gone well past a viable threat—which admittedly we have—to a world-wide pandemic."

Aiden shook his head. "If my gut is right, we just opened Pandora's box."

TWO

Clad in a head-to-toe protective hazmat suit, Rachel Allen slowed her breathing to match the rate of the respirator mounted on her belt. With each exhale of the purified air pumped into her helmet, lip-shaped condensation formed on her acrylic face mask.

"Dr. Moreno, I don't understand the rush," she said to her boss who was suited up and impatient for her to finish taping her gloves to her suit so that she could follow him into the Level 4 biocontainment lab. "You know that whatever this—virus—is, it's going to take time to analyze."

"I know." He waved her on. "I've spent the past twenty-four hours doing just that."

"Wait a minute. . .Is that why I'm here?" she asked. "Were your results inconclusive?"

Dr. Moreno hesitated, clearly not wanting to give her the entire picture. "Not inconclusive, but I need a second opinion."

"Of course. You know I'm always willing to help—"

"Just remember, this is a time-sensitive sample. Level one priority."

She wanted to say *obviously, from the crazy way you're behaving*, but instead she said, "I've cleared my schedule for the next forty-eight hours as you requested."

"Good."

9

Once the negative pressure registered that the lab door had sealed behind them, Dr. Moreno flipped on the light to the biosafety hood. Four vials glittered in the rack behind a protective glass front.

He turned to Rachel, his breath inside his helmet fogging his glasses. "I'm sorry you'll miss the fundraiser tonight."

Rachel shrugged. She hadn't wanted to go, and now she had a legitimate excuse. Swanky parties always made her feel like an unwanted virus trying to gain access to a stubborn host cell. Maybe she could return the cocktail dress and strappy heels her colleague, Cara, had insisted she buy last weekend.

"Okay by me," Rachel assured him. "I'm not good at rubbing elbows."

"This stays between us, Dr. Allen, agreed?"

Rachel's brow furrowed. "What stays between us?"

"Everything." He waved his gloved hand at the vials. "About *this*."

Still not clear as to why her boss had summoned her to his office, instructed her to suit up, and then locked the two of them inside Gaumond Labs' highest-level biocontainment lab, Rachel pressed for answers. "What is. . .*this*?"

Dr. Moreno's furtive gaze traveled the negative pressure room as if searching for hidden cameras, then he leaned in. "Construction of a Tibetan railroad uncovered what we believe to be an ancient virus buried beneath the permafrost. A friend of mine asked me to test the samples they found in ice cores drilled from the glacier."

"Did the researchers use decontamination protocols?"

"They did everything by the book."

"So what exactly are you looking for?"

"I need you to confirm the virus's viability."

Rachel laughed. "Viability?"

She stopped laughing when her boss's eyes narrowed behind his mask, suddenly grateful her protective gear had muffled the depth of her scoffing skepticism. But still. . .

"Surely you told whoever sent this virus that has been dead and frozen for decades, if not centuries, that it cannot be thawed and brought back to life?"

Her boss eyed her then slowly shook his head.

"Dr. Moreno, you and I both know that to even propose the possibility is science fiction, not real science."

"Yes, but there are exceptions to every rule. In 2016, an anthrax outbreak was attributed to melting permafrost in Siberia."

"The deaths of those reindeer were never definitively linked to the revival of dormant anthrax. Even if it were proven that climate change had activated long-buried spores, anthrax is bacterial not viral," Rachel argued despite knowing Dr. Moreno had forgotten more about the pathology of dangerous pathogens than she would ever know. "They don't play by the same rules."

"If you can't handle this unique advancement opportunity, Dr. Allen, then I'll assign this job to someone else."

His insistence they waste time on a scientific improbability had her puzzled, but his threat of stalling her career made her blood boil. She'd put off marriage and family for the sake of proving herself capable of carving out a place in the medical field that would garner the respect her father and brother had achieved. Besides, what was another night in the lab?

"That won't be necessary." She clenched her fists. "Viruses are my sole focus."

"I know. That's why I'm bringing you into this." If her decision to forgo a private life impressed him, it did not register on his face. "Use protozoa and primate cells."

"Both?" The absurdity flew from her lips. "If you want this ancient virus to resurrect itself, primate cells are a waste of time. Few modern viruses are capable of replicating in both."

"Dr. Allen. . ." He hesitated as if searching for the words to explain. "Not only are you confirming viability of the virus, but you are testing to confirm or deny its ability to jump to humans."

"This is crazy."

His frustration and anxiety were evident on his face. "I hope you're right, but there *is* evidence it's already made the jump."

Rachel's mind spun around the improbability. The man might have lost perspective for the sake of the friend who'd sent him down this rabbit hole, but he had her attention. "When?"

"That's all I can tell you at this point." Dr. Moreno handed her a small spiral notebook. "Write down all your findings and bring them directly to me when you're finished. I have responsibilities for tonight's function that would be questioned if I didn't show up. Otherwise, I would stay right here. Understand?"

Normally, everything they did was meticulously tracked with computerized data management software. Never by scribbled notes on a page. Without a digital footprint, the notebook could disappear along with whatever she'd discovered. It would be his word against hers.

"Perfectly." Rachel waited for the click of the slamming door's airlock before she slid her triple-gloved hands inside the biosafety cabinet. Viruses needed a living host to survive. There was no way for a virus that had been languishing for centuries in frozen tundra to thaw then suddenly spring to life.

Then why were her hands shaking?

She was used to working with exotic strains of flu, SARS, MERS, plague, Ebola, Marburg. She'd even done a wide range study of bioterrorism pathogens like tularemia, Q fever, and melioidosis. Being terrified of a dead virus, no matter how much havoc it had dealt the world thousands of years ago, was crazy. Dead viruses did not miraculously resurrect. Even if climate change continued to melt the earth's permafrost, the world was at far greater risk from the release of all of the carbon dioxide and methane stored beneath the icy crust than the awakening of killer Zombie viruses.

But no matter how ridiculous she considered this assignment, her training would not allow her to step outside of the safety regulation protocols imposed upon a Level B4 lab.

Rachel took a deep breath then glanced at the handwritten label on the package sitting on the counter next to her that had held the vials.

Dr. Aiden Ballinger.

Seeing the familiar name of the world's foremost virus hunter surprised her. She regularly followed his YouTube channel and had read every article the acclaimed explorer had ever written about his enviable and dangerous scientific adventures in remote locations. A man who'd worked so hard to acquire such a renowned body of work would not risk his reputation on a scientific impossibility. Dr. Moreno had hinted this virus had already been confirmed viable by the sender. But what kind of proof did Dr. Ballinger have? What kind of tests had he run? Who was sick, and why did he think the cause could be traced to this virus?

She held one of the thumb-sized vials to the light, needing confirmation that her boss's fears were valid. The contents looked innocent, incapable of causing harm. Her jangled nerves steadied.

From a wire rack inside a liquid nitrogen container, Rachel carefully extracted a test tube. Inside the glass vial, a sheet of green monkey kidney cells coated the tube's interior surface. She seeded the primate cells with a drop of the ancient virus then noted the procedure, the cell line used, and the *one PM* start time in Dr. Moreno's notebook. Virus incubation periods varied anywhere from eight hours to years, but she was unwilling to leave these specific results to chance. She set the timer, sprayed her gloves with disinfectant, then wheeled her stool over to the computer.

Between checking the progress of the virus over the next four hours and recording the data, she googled Dr. Ballinger. She could confirm his team had been in Tibet, but if he'd discovered something deadly, he was uncharacteristically quiet.

When the timer alarm finally dinged, Rachel wheeled back to the biohood. If she was going to shut down the ridiculous notion that an ancient virus could infect humans, she might as well start with the primate tube. She dipped a sterile swab into the vial then smeared a sterile glass slide with the cells. She placed the sample under the lens of a low magnification inverted microscope.

A gasp clouded her mask. Heart rate accelerating, she fiddled with the focus control.

Dark aggregated blotches indicated molecular changes inside the monkey cells. Not only had an ancient giant virus awakened, in less than four hours it had proven its ability to replicate in vertebrates. A virus that could so quickly and efficiently break the barrier walls of healthy cells was a virus that might be able to break the barriers between animals and humans. Any virus with this kind of adaptability was a virus that must be contained.

Is this what Dr. Moreno had found that had him so clearly shaken?

Dr. Moreno had made himself clear that her findings were not to be shared via email or text, but she wasn't willing to trust this shocking information to a notebook.

Rachel capped the vial of remaining monkey cells. She removed the slide from the microscope then sterilized everything. She slipped into the shower room and washed her suit beneath the sensor-activated chemical disinfectant showerheads. With the initial shower finished, she doffed her suit in the outer changing room, disposed of her protective scrubs, gloves, and socks in a biohazard container, showered her body head to toe with HydroClens, then quickly toweled and dressed in her street clothes.

Using her ID on the electronic pad, she locked the lab behind her and hurried to her boss's office. When he didn't answer the door, she checked the handle. Locked. She peered through the small glass window. Dark.

A tap on the shoulder caused Rachel to jump with a start then wheel. "Cara, you scared me to death!"

Rachel's friend and fellow lab tech was dressed in a sexy red cocktail dress. "Come on, I don't want to be late."

"For what?"

"The meet and greet. Remember?" Cara thrust into Rachel's arms the royal-blue, knee-length dress she'd forced Rachel to buy last weekend. "I got this from your office, but you need to hurry. Who knows how long it will take us to get across DC during rush hour."

Water dripped from Rachel's wet hair onto the gauzy fabric. The small drops quickly spread into wide overlapping circles, as if replicating themselves like the giant virus she'd just seen on the slide. How could she go to a party when there was a potential monster growing in her lab?

Rachel shoved the dress back into Cara's arms. "I'm going to have to skip the party. I need to find Dr. Moreno."

"Now?"

"Yes, now." Rachel instantly regretted her harsh tone, but she couldn't exactly give a full explanation.

"Dr. Moreno's already left for the fundraiser. In fact, he's been in meetings with potential investors all afternoon."

"I know funding's important, but—"

"Don't even think you're going to get out of this." Cara jammed a balled fist on her narrow waist. "I know you prefer a hot date with one of your enthralling virus textbooks and a microwave dinner, but girl, you need to get out."

How was she supposed to keep this assignment under wraps and get the help she needed without setting off her co-worker's keen senses? "Look, Cara—"

"You need to have some fun."

"I have plenty of fun."

"Then maybe you should tell your face—because you look stressed."

"I'm not stressed." Rachel forced a smile. "I just really need to talk to him."

Cara's gaze scoured Rachel's oversized sweatshirt, leggings, and tennis shoes. "Then you'll have to come to the party."

Rachel snatched the dress back from Cara, out of options. "Give me ten minutes."

As the Uber driver wove through the Capitol's rush hour traffic, Cara plied Rachel with lip gloss and questions about her top-secret project. Nearly out of diversions, Rachel was relieved when their car finally pulled into the artfully lit circle drive of the Au-Tenleytown home.

Two valets opened their doors, and the women got out.

Cara's wide-eyed gaze traveled up the steps that led to the sparkling glass doors of the stone mansion. "Welcome to the land of the one percent, missionary girl," she whispered to Rachel.

For a moment, Rachel wished she'd taken her big brother's advice and not told anyone about growing up in the Amazon jungle. But she was proud of what her father had accomplished, despite the fact that bringing healing and hope to a forgotten people had cost him his life. Her father's willingness to look beyond himself was the number one factor behind her own decision to follow in his medical footsteps. She was much more comfortable sitting around a cooking fire in a remote Columbian village than at a fancy urban party, but people could die if she allowed herself to be intimidated by a mountain of architectural stone and beveled glass.

Rachel tucked away her secret intent as if it were a dried curl that had escaped the messy bun she'd twisted atop her head. "Let's find Dr. Moreno."

Cara rolled her eyes at the improbability of Rachel loosening up enough to have fun. "Let's find the bar."

"You have fun your way. I'll have fun my way." Rachel stepped around her friend and rang the doorbell.

A man wearing a black tux and white gloves ushered them into a foyer bigger than the hospital lobby where Rachel had done her residency in epidemiology, then relieved them of their coats.

"I'm thirsty." Cara took Rachel by the elbow. "Let's find the champagne."

"You should go easy. We've got to work tomorrow."

"Not everyone works twenty-four-seven, you know."

"I'll catch up." Rachel pulled herself free. "After I find Dr. Moreno."

"Have you always been such a good girl?"

"Just OCD. Can't move on until all of the puzzle pieces fit."

Cara sighed. "You're hopeless." She turned and started drifting through the crowd decked out in glittery dresses and black tuxes. Members of Washington's most connected and influential circles clustered around pub tables decorated with heavy linens and candles floating in glass vases filled with water.

Rachel rose on the tiptoes of her high heels and searched for Dr. Moreno's distinguished gray hair.

"You look as uncomfortable as an unwanted genome in a virus." The deep male voice behind her caused Rachel to pivot with a start.

The familiarity of the reference was nearly as attractive as the man with Ryan Gosling good looks behind tortoise-shell glasses and the perfect low-maintenance Ivy League haircut. Rugged stubble framed a confident smile that proclaimed he had better things to do with his time than primp. His crew neck white T-shirt, dark jeans, tweed jacket, and lace-up boots declared him independent of what anyone thought.

"D-Dr. Ballinger?" she stuttered.

"Yeah, how did you know?"

Even though she could feel his smoldering dark eyes examining her with the laser-sharp focus of a high-powered microscope, something about him put her immediately at ease. "I subscribe to your YouTube channel and have read everything you've ever written."

His smile revealed a set of perfect white teeth. "You need a life."

She liked him. Which was ridiculous, because she'd just met him. And on top of that, attraction was a dangerous thing for a woman with career aspirations. "They don't let me out of the lab that often."

"I can see why." His intensity sent a surge of warmth spreading through Rachel's core. "Your charm could be fatal if released on the world."

Their conversation had definitely taken a turn toward the geeky, but it held a sexy quality she found irresistible.

She knew better than to trust a stranger, even one she'd stalked extensively, but something about him caused her normal defenses to slip. She could recite where he'd gotten his degrees, how he liked his tea when he was camping at a remote site, plus the names of every virus he'd hunted down.

"Does that line work with most women?" she asked.

"First time to use it," he admitted with a chuckle.

"Sounds like I'm not the only one who needs a life." Before she could ask why he was in DC, Cara pushed between them, a glass of champagne in hand.

"Aiden! I can't believe you're here," she gushed. "I haven't seen you since residency."

"Cara!" He gave Rachel's giddy colleague a quick hug then held her at arm's length. "You look great."

"Is that still your best line, Ballinger?" Cara laughed.

Aiden cast Rachel a questioning glance. When she kept their conversation to herself, he smiled. "Guess so."

Cara shook her head. "Once an absent-minded science nerd, always an absent-minded science nerd." She emptied her champagne glass then waved for another. She was halfway through her drink when she realized Aiden and Rachel were staring at each other. "I didn't know the two of you had met."

"Not officially," Rachel said. "I've followed his career from the sidelines."

"Let me introduce you to your hero." Cara took another sip of her drink. "Dr. Rachel Allen, meet Dr. Aiden Ballinger, the—"

"The virus hunter." Rachel wasn't embarrassed by the admiration in her voice. This guy had earned it.

Cara draped one arm over Aiden's shoulder. "Aiden's the Indiana Jones of our little world of obscure viruses."

Aiden's gaze held Rachel captive. "Believe me, tramping around in permafrost while your fingers are turning blue isn't that romantic." He smiled at her. "The real heroes are the people who figure out how to keep the viruses I dig up from replicating."

Rachel's gut clenched. It was too late. That cage had already been opened. "Why are you in DC, Dr. Ballinger?"

"Aiden," he corrected. "I needed a second opinion on some findings in the field."

"Sounds intriguing," Cara said.

"Hardly." Aiden stuffed his hands in his pants pockets. "Just a bunch of boring lab work."

Rachel stopped herself from saying she knew exactly what the *boring* lab work entailed. Maybe that's why Dr. Ballinger had come to the party. Maybe he knew her boss would be here.

"So you know Dr. Moreno?" Rachel asked Aiden, fishing for more information.

"Yeah, I was hoping to speak to him tonight."

"Me too, actually," Rachel said.

"But we haven't been able to find him." Cara sipped her drink. "Not that I've been looking that hard."

"You both work at Gaumond Labs?" Aiden asked.

"We do." Cara set her teetering champagne glass on the nearest table. "Time to liven up this party. Whoever spots Dr. Moreno first, send off a flare."

Cara wheeled and wobbled off, leaving Rachel and Aiden standing face to face. Rachel ran through her options as she felt his eyes on her.

"Cara hasn't changed," he said, taking a step closer. "Look, I'm here to—"

He didn't have to tell her why he was here because she already knew. "I have your results," she whispered.

His eyes widened. "And?"

"If we're going to save the world, we need to find Dr. Moreno ASAP."

THREE

You look as uncomfortable as an unwanted genome in a virus?

Aiden studied the blonde standing in front of him and felt his brow begin to perspire. Seriously? Had he actually said that to her? What stunned him the most was that she hadn't run. But trying to impress the beautiful woman who'd already managed to captivate him wasn't why he was here. And definitely wasn't the biggest problem he was facing at the moment. He hadn't missed the concern in her voice. She was the brilliant virus expert Dr. Moreno had promised to have double check the test results. The sooner he had reliable data, the sooner his team could initiate the response needed to shut down the growing death rate in Tibet.

He cupped her elbow as he led her to the edge of the crowded room. "I need to know what you found in that lab."

"Sorry." She shook her head. "I have specific orders not to talk to anyone."

"Those were *my* instructions." He pulled his hand away from her and lowered his voice. "Those vials your lab received were from me."

"I'm aware of that, but still—"

"If you know anything about viruses—which I'm assuming you do—then I don't have to tell you about the dangers that come with the reemergence of a high-consequence pathogen for which there are no vaccines or cures. In the wrong hands, a reactivated virus could spread across the globe like a wildfire and kill millions."

"Wait a minute. . ." She held up her hand, refusing to buy into his paranoia. "Don't you think you're getting ahead of yourself? All we have is a viable virus with evidence it can spread to humans."

"Isn't that enough?" he asked.

"I'm going to need to see more evidence before I jump to the conclusion that this virus you discovered is going to turn into a. . .a pandemic."

Aiden frowned. Yes, he'd heard that before, but still, this was not the scenario he'd envisioned. "Did your results confirm that the virus is related to the outbreak?"

"From the notes I read, yes."

"How long did it take for the virus to replicate in vertebrates?"

She hesitated. "Four hours, but—"

"Four hours. It should have taken twice that long. Actually, it never should have happened at all, because that virus shouldn't have been viable, but it was. It is. And now you just confirmed that I'm not crazy."

"I never said you were crazy, but the probability of. . ." She glanced around. "I shouldn't even be talking about this with you. I—"

"You can see how serious this is."

Her frown deepened. "Do you always interrupt people, or just when you're not getting your way?"

"I'm sorry." He bit back his frustration that wasn't targeted on her, but the entire situation. "All I know is that my resources in the field were limited. I was able to run the tests more than once, but my team needs clarification if we're going to have a decent shot at setting up the proper protocols. That's why I came to Dr. Moreno."

"I agree that the initial results are surprising, but we have to do more testing. What we have so far doesn't seem much worse than a bad case of the flu."

"We are now looking at over fifty suspected cases, and five deaths."

"Which is my point exactly." Rachel leaned toward him while the party buzzed around them. "Suspected. . .possible. . .up to. . .none of these words are scientific. You, of all people, know that."

"My team can determine the reproduction number once we can

compare all the data. The death rate for the flu is typically less than one percent. What we're seeing in the Tibetan village is significantly higher."

"Knowing the average number of people who catch the virus from a single infected person is important, but I still think you're jumping way ahead of yourself. We don't have enough data."

"My job is to study high-consequence pathogens, and I'm telling you I've never seen anything this reactive." He glanced behind her to the party where music was playing and waiters were handing out food and drinks. "My boss told me to meet him and Moreno here."

Aiden studied the crowd again. A room full of lab geeks, directors from the board, and backers all mingling and laughing over who knows what. But like Rachel, he hadn't seen Dr. Moreno or Nick Shepherd. But he did spot Cara making her way back toward them. Something told him they needed to ensure she didn't get looped into the discussion.

"I don't see my boss." He grabbed Rachel's elbow again and steered her toward the door. "If your boss isn't here, where would he be?"

"Let me try him again." Rachel called Moreno's number, then frowned. "I've called him half a dozen times and he's still not picking up."

"What about his wife?"

"She should be here."

He searched the crowd again, glad to see that Cara had been snagged into another conversation.

"There she is," Rachel said.

They headed across the large room toward the front door where Teresa Moreno was chatting with a petite redhead.

"Teresa. . .you look stunning," Aiden said as soon as the redhead vanished into the crowd.

"Good to see you, Aiden." Teresa cocked her head slightly. "I didn't know the two of you knew each other."

"We don't," Rachel said. "Not really. I've just followed his career."

"I don't blame you. He's quite impressive." Teresa turned to Aiden. "Joel told me you were in town. I expect you to come by the house. It looks like you could use a home-cooked meal."

"You know I'd love that."

"Good. I'll have Joel nail down a date with you. I have to do everything around his schedule."

"What we really need," Rachel said, "is your husband. We haven't seen him."

"Join the club. He's been in meetings all afternoon and is running late as usual. I got a text from him about an hour ago. He had to go back to the lab for something, but promised he'd meet me here." Teresa frowned. "How can someone so precise in the lab not give the same careful attention to his watch? Honestly, I'd decided if he didn't show up in the next ten minutes, I was going home."

"He probably lost track of time," Aiden said.

Teresa rested her hand on Aiden's arm. "Is everything all right?"

"Of course." He glanced at Rachel. "We're working on a project together, and we need to ask him a few questions. But it can wait. I know he's busy."

"If you'll excuse me," Teresa said, grabbing an avocado bruschetta off a silver tray, "I have one more person I need to talk to before I head out."

Rachel turned back to Aiden. "What do you think?"

"Maybe Moreno went to meet my boss at your lab."

"I'll text Cara that I'm leaving."

A minute later they'd collected their coats and were heading down the long driveway toward his car in the forty-something-degree January weather. He clicked his key fob and the lights of his silver compact car flashed. He opened the passenger door, waited for her to get settled, then hurried around to the driver's side. A few seconds later, he had the car running and the struggling heater turned full blast. He eased around the expensive vehicles parked in the driveway then floored it. Maybe he was overreacting, but being wrong wasn't a chance he was willing to take.

Aiden cut a glance at the woman sitting next to him as he sped down the expressway toward Alexandria. The entire situation was ironic. Here he was, alone with a beautiful woman who was wearing a stunning dress and heels. Instead of getting to know each other over fancy hors d'oeuvres, they were headed to a biocontainment lab. He'd meant what he said. He did need to get out more, but his work was the main reason he rarely dated. Spending months out in the field and not knowing when he would be coming home wasn't exactly the stable kind of relationship most women wanted. In fact, right now the closest thing he could call home was his current hotel room. That didn't exactly scream stability.

Twenty minutes later, he pulled into the underground garage next to the lab and parked. A surveillance camera light flashed in the corner.

"Dr. Moreno's car is here." Rachel opened the passenger door and climbed out. "He's probably in the lab checking my work, or in his office planning to fire me for leaving after he told me not to."

She used her security pass to get them inside the building then headed directly to the third floor. "We'll try his office first." A minute later she stopped at one of the doors and started to knock.

"That's odd." She inclined her head toward the partially open door. "He never leaves his office unlocked. Dr. Moreno?" She stepped inside the room then stopped. "Aiden?"

At the alarm in her voice, Aiden quickly pushed past her. Something caught his eye, and he walked over to the edge of the desk. There was blood smeared on the corner and a puddle of red on the floor. Nausea swept through him as his mind zoomed in on the possibilities. "Rachel. . .Where's the virus?"

FOUR

Aiden tried to pull her away from the bloody edge of the desk when she didn't respond. "Where's the virus, Rachel?"

The voice imploring her to move sounded garbled, as if her head were held underwater, but her feet refused to give in and follow the urgent tug on her wrist.

"Rachel." Aiden spun her around, and his grip on her shoulders tightened. "We have to make sure the virus is secure. Where is it?"

"There has to be a reasonable explanation for the blood. Like Dr. Moreno tripped or. . .or maybe the blood belongs to someone on the nightly cleaning crew."

Her brother Josiah was constantly accusing her of making a mountain out of a mole hill. Before she jumped to the worst-case scenario, she needed information.

She tried to refocus her attention to the cell phone in her hand. They should call someone. Security? The police? Dr. Moreno's wife? Yes. That made the most sense. Before she set off any false alarms, she should ask Teresa if her husband had called her to say he'd been hurt. But if Dr. Moreno had cut himself with a broken lab vial, he wouldn't have called his wife to tell her he'd possibly been exposed to a high-consequence pathogen. And even if he'd been working in a Level 2 lab, which he rarely did, he wouldn't have left a sealed environment to go bleed all over his desk. He would have followed the lab's well-defined and well-rehearsed protocols for exposure to any type of virus, dangerous or not, and immediately alerted the facility manager.

Aiden's eyes bored into hers. "Rachel, listen to me. I know you have a lot of questions, but you've got to trust me. We need to make sure the virus is safe, or this whole thing could get a whole lot worse."

Worse? How could things possibly get worse?

"I don't have to trust you." She pulled free of his hold and took a step back. "I just met you. I can see that something is very wrong here. My boss is missing, there's blood all over his desk, and there's a viable super virus in the building that presumably can start a worldwide pandemic, according to you. But you. . .I don't really know you."

"Look." He raised his palms and calmed his voice. "Joel knew the risks when he agreed to secretly look at this for me—"

"That's the problem. Why all the secrecy? Dr. Moreno said the same thing, and even insisted I write my notes in a cheap spiral instead of logging them digitally. Yes, I saw how that virus reacted in the lab, but nothing about the way we're handling this is how I've been trained to handle things at Gaumond Labs."

"I'll explain everything once I've made sure the sample is safe."

"No." Her hands clenched into fists. "You'll explain everything now. From the beginning."

He took a frustrated breath, leaned in like he didn't want anyone to overhear, and whispered, "I brought the samples to Joel. One had cells I'd taken from the heart of a dead twenty-year-old Tibetan woman. The other was virus cells recovered from the heart of the original suspected host. I can't lose those samples."

"It's not the end of the world if you have to go back to Tibet to procure other samples."

"I can't." He raked his fingers through his hair. "Traditional Tibetans give their loved ones a sky burial. The dead disappear within hours."

She'd read about the practice of allowing harsh mountain elements and predatory animals to return a dead body to the earth. "What about the virus host?"

"The virus host was a frozen baby woolly mammoth discovered deep in the permafrost."

"Why did Dr. Moreno tell me the virus came from core samples drilled from the ice?"

"Because that's what I asked him to say." He took a breath. "Hear me out, please."

"This better be good."

"We lost solar power up on the mountain. Without the power, our extra samples decomposed rapidly."

"Surely you took more host samples than the single vial we received."

"My priority was to get the host and victim samples to Joel ASAP. It took five hours on horseback to come off the mountain. Then another two hours of navigating switchbacks in a jeep to get to the nearest landing strip. By the time I had phone service again, it was too late to do anything about the text I'd gotten from Iceman."

"Iceman?"

"Colleague and old college roommate. He was in Tibet with me."

"What did his text say?"

"We lost the mammoth too."

"Oh, no." Rachel was warming to the truth of his story, but from what she'd seen of the capabilities of this virus today, she knew she couldn't be too cautious. "So the vials in our lab are the only uncompromised sample of what you found?"

He swallowed. "Yes, and trust me, if you saw what I saw when I autopsied that mammoth, you would want to make sure this virus doesn't spread."

From what little she'd already seen of this giant virus's aggressive ability to replicate, she wouldn't be surprised if it possessed Herculean destructive capabilities. "What did you see?"

"That prehistoric little elephant had suffered from having his entire heart riddled with huge wormholes."

"Some sort of adenovirus?" she asked.

"Maybe. But from the look on your face, I think you agree this doesn't act like any other heart virus you've seen before."

"It would take more testing before I could say definitively what this virus could or could not do to a heart." She took in a measured breath, wishing she could slow her racing heart. "I have a close friend I could call. No one knows hearts like Mia Kendall. She might be able to help of make sense of the virus and its symptoms—"

"No," Aiden said before she could finish her sentence. "We can't trust anyone. Not with everything that's happened."

"We can trust her—"

"Even if we could, I'm not willing to drag someone else into this and put their life potentially at risk. We need more information. There's a possibility someone came for the sample, and they weren't willing to wait for Joel to agree to give it to them."

"Are you proposing some sort of government conspiracy stuff?"

"Maybe." His gaze shifted to the floor. "But I still haven't told you everything."

Rachel rubbed at the intense pounding between her eyes, unsure at the moment what she should believe. "I'm listening."

"When I'm out in the field, I have to rely on digital communications to transmit my findings and data. Unfortunately, there are vulnerabilities in the systems. Hackers interested in collecting the information I'm gathering."

"What kind of information?"

"All my stats on the virus," he said. "I contacted a friend who's big into high tech. Long story short, he was able to find malware apps running in the background and sending information back to an unknown server. If the specifics of this virus were to get into the wrong hands, the results could be deadly."

"The only reason someone would want a Level 4 virus is"—her head snapped up— "to weaponize it."

Aiden's slight nod sent a wave of terror coursing through her. "That's exactly what I'm trying to say. We've already seen a small sampling of what it can do in its raw form. Imagine if its deadliest components are maximized."

Rachel let her gaze slide from Aiden to the corner of the desk. The world was not ready for a virus like this. "We need to look at the security tape."

"You have access?"

She nodded, then slid into the chair in front of Dr. Moreno's desk, typed in her password, then scrolled to the closed-circuit recording. She ran the tape back a few minutes, then stopped as a large man dressed completely in black and a ball cap pushed Dr. Moreno out of his office. Blood ran down Dr. Moreno's head as the man forced him down the hallway and onto the elevator. Rachel could see the word *security* written on the back of the aggressor's jacket and a Gaumond Labs' patch on his left arm.

"I don't recognize that guard," she said.

"I don't think that's a Gaumond guard."

She started clicking through more of the footage, searching for where they'd taken Moreno.

"There." Aiden tapped on the screen as they appeared again. "Where are they going?"

"It's a separate research wing." She paused the footage again. "Moreno must be trying to stall him."

Aiden's cell phone buzzed. His frown deepened as he read the message.

"We might have another problem." He held out his cell phone.

She took it and read the text.

THERE'S MORE GOING ON HERE THAN JUST A DEADLY VIRUS. I THINK SOMEONE IS AFTER ME. INSIDE JOB. NOT SAFE. DON'T KNOW WHO TO TRUST. WATCH YOUR BACK.

She handed the phone back to Aiden, panic now raging full force. "Who's this from?"

"My boss," Aiden said, and quickly placed a call. "Come on, Shepherd. Answer me." He stared at the phone as the call switched to voice message. Aiden grabbed her hand. "We need to get the virus out of here."

Rachel shook her head. "The safest place for the virus is right where it is in our Level 4 lab."

"Not if this is an inside job." Aiden caught her gaze. "Not if someone uses Moreno to get into the lab."

Rachel swallowed hard, terrified at the thought. She knew Moreno. If someone was trying to force him to hand over the virus, he'd do everything in his power to stop them, but what if he didn't succeed? What if the virus ended up in the wrong hands?

"We need to get to the lab."

She could almost feel Aiden's breath on the back of her neck as he followed her through the large multi-story atrium that separated the office spaces from the BSL-4 laboratories.

The elevator slipped past the floor with the deserted workout facility, and finally past the floor that housed the cook tanks where liquid waste from the lab sinks and showers was autoclaved. By the time they reached the basement level, Rachel still didn't have a plan to stop this rulebreaker from taking what he claimed was his.

"This it?" Aiden's calm voice cut through the storm in her head.

"Yes."

They stepped into the wide, well-lit, and eerily quiet hallway. She'd spent many nights in this facility, but she'd never felt afraid. She was always locked inside the lab where she'd stay until her need for morning coffee drove her stumbling into the next shift of researchers. This pin-drop quiet must be what had her spooked, because her trembling hands were having trouble fishing her ID badge out of her purse.

She held her picture up to the electronic pad that opened the door. Access granted, she hurried through the corridor that led to the solid concrete box lab where she'd foolishly left a potential ancient killer unattended.

Long banks of windows faced both sides of the hall. The transparency had two purposes. If researchers could see out, it helped reduce the claustrophobic feeling that came with being sealed inside a locked room. If management could see in, the sense of being watched increased accountability and reduced mistakes.

Rachel cupped her hands to the glass outside her Level 4 lab. The room had the faint red glow cast by the exit sign above the door to her right, but it was too dark inside to see if anything had been disturbed. She checked the negative air pressure readings on the lighted panel beside the lab's outer door. If anyone had opened the inner door after she'd left for the party, the system had restabilized.

"Everything looks normal." Rachel leaned her face toward the tiny iris scanner. A click sounded and the automatic door lock released. "We need to hurry." She led Aiden into the clothing room. "You can wear your glasses, but no other personal items are allowed." She pointed at the stacks of surgical scrubs, socks, and underwear.

"Not exactly Calvin Klein," he said.

"Safety trumps comfort."

"Disposable underwear's a luxury for a guy who just spent the past few weeks living in a tent."

She felt her cheeks flame, then turned without comment and gathered what they needed. "This way." They stepped inside the small locker room. "You can use that changing closet." She took the other one. She kicked off her heels and slid out of her fancy cocktail dress. A few minutes later, she was clad in scratchy paper underwear and cotton scrubs. The low-grade quality had never bothered her before, but it grated against her skin as if Aiden Ballinger had awakened every nerve in her body.

Once they were both dressed, they passed into a room where different sizes of hazmat suits hung from the drying rack. She helped Aiden pick the one most likely to fit his six-foot lean and muscular frame. She inflated the suit with an air hose hanging from the ceiling then listened for leaks. He did the same for her once she was safely sealed inside her suit. Aiden held her wrist and taped her triple layer of gloves to each sleeve of her suit with the skill of someone who'd done this a million times. She was relieved he didn't break rules when it came to lab protocol, but his touch was a dangerous fire she could feel through all the protective layers. Her hands were still trembling as she taped his gloves.

She returned the tape to the storage bin. "Ready for a helmet?"

"You first." He removed the helmet from the rack with the word *Allen* written across the back. "This one yours?"

She nodded.

He leaned in so close his breath brushed her cheek as he placed the clear bubble over her head. She sucked in a gulp of the oxygen flowing into her mask and reined in her thoughts. "Our suits are equipped with a fully functional communication system. We can talk to each other in the lab or communicate with people outside the lab."

"Great," he said. "I'll order a pizza. See if they can get it delivered before we catch this virus and die."

"I meant, if Dr. Moreno found a way to contact me."

His grin slid from his lips. "You don't break rules and you don't joke, right?"

Her brother Josiah accused her of having no sense of humor. After their father died, Josiah had been the one who'd used humor to deflect his pain. Although it had frustrated her older brother that he could never get his little sister to lighten up, it hadn't stopped him from trying. Her brother was the only man left in her life who truly loved her, and because of that, his constant teasing and joking was a trait she'd grown to appreciate and admire. But it wasn't a trait she'd ever managed to imitate.

"You're the one claiming someone wants to wipe out humanity." She couldn't let the fact that this man was alarmingly handsome, intriguing, and somewhat funny distract her. "Doesn't that feel serious to you? Because it feels serious to me." She slid a clear helmet over his sandy brown hair. Behind the lens of his glasses, his intelligent eyes watched every movement she made with more than a clinical interest in whether or not she'd done everything properly.

"I say stupid things when I'm nervous," he admitted.

"That makes two of us." She snapped his helmet latches securely in place then turned toward the door and palmed a large rubber switch designed to open the first door of the airlock. "If someone broke the seal on the second door, this door won't open." She kept her eyes on the last barrier between them and the possibility of a horrendous death if Aiden's concerns were real and someone had managed to breach the safety measures and gain entrance to the lab. Handling test tubes filled with a deadly pathogen was like handling nitroglycerin; the slightest misstep could set the virus free. The gasket seals released, the heavy door swung open, and the automatic lights flickered on.

Rachel scanned the lab. The computer was dark. The biosafety cabinet appeared undisturbed. And to her relief, the door to the freezer where she'd stored the vials was shut.

She stepped across the threshold. "We need to hurry. We might have got here first, but they could arrive any minute."

Aiden followed her. "Specimens in freezer?"

"Yes."

He went to the freezer, stuck his gloved hand in, and pulled out the rack. "Where do you keep your insulated shipping containers?"

"Second cabinet to your right. I'll grab the slow-melt ice packs out of the bigger freezer."

A metal tray clanged on the floor as she returned with the packs a moment later. Rachel jumped with a start.

"Found it." Aiden held up a small cooler.

"If you plan to store that virus for a long period of time, we should consider adding FBS to raise the serum concentration to a final level of twenty percent."

"Good idea."

To reduce the loss of the virus's infectivity, she opted to pack the O-ring vials on wet ice. She sealed the cooler and taped it shut for good measure, then held up the tidy package as if she'd just boxed his leftovers. "Where do you plan to take them?"

"I'm still working on that plan."

"You're going to have to come up with something fast. We're only going to have seventy-two hours of guaranteed virus viability at this point," she said heading back toward the shower room in front of him.

Two minutes later, he stepped out with a towel around his waist. "Need help out of your suit?" he asked.

"I've got it." She handed him the package then disappeared into the chemical steam and shut the door. Five minutes later, she was dressed once again in her cocktail dress and heels. She fingered the tangles from her wet hair and went to meet Aiden.

Rachel held her badge to the hallway door and it opened. They stepped into the hall. They were halfway to the elevator when the doors opened. Aiden quickly pulled Rachel into a small alcove and out of sight.

"Can you see who it is?" she asked.

Aiden peeked around the corner. "It's the security guard from the video, but this time he's alone."

She pressed her back against the wall, trying to slow her breathing.

So where was Moreno?

"Is there a back door out of here?" Aiden whispered.

"There's an emergency exit two floors up. We can take the stairs."

Aiden grabbed her hand. "It might be too late. He's coming toward us."

FIVE

There's more going on here than just a deadly virus.

Aiden pressed his back against the wall and hugged the insulated container to his chest. Footsteps echoed against the tile as the armed man they'd seen on the security footage headed straight toward where they were hiding. His boss's words kept running through his mind, but he was trying not to think about Shepherd's warning, or what might have happened to Dr. Moreno. His biggest concern at the moment was getting Rachel safely out of here.

A cell phone rang and the footsteps coming toward them paused.

Aiden held his breath, waiting for the other man to make his next move. A moment later, footsteps sounded again, but this time they were heading away from them. They needed to move. Now.

"What's the fastest way out of this building?" Aiden whispered.

"Stairs to our left."

He let out a sharp breath then peeked around the corner to make sure the coast was clear. The man had turned back toward the elevators and was deeply involved in his phone conversation. Aiden squeezed her fingers, signaling for them to move. His initial plan was simple. All they had to do was get to his car in the parking garage, then get as far away from here as possible. After that they could figure out how to get some answers.

Rachel stopped in front of a door, her hands shaking as she slid her badge across the access strip.

A red light flashed.

"What's wrong?" Aiden asked.

"I don't know." She swiped it again. "Come on, come on. . ."

Aiden glanced in the direction of the elevators, feeling exposed. He couldn't see the face of the security guard, but he could still hear him talking on his phone. If the guy finished his call and decided to turn back, he'd see them.

A second later, the green light came on, and the door clicked open.

"Two floors up, there's a fire door that leads outside," she said, easing the door open and slipping inside. "From there we can get to the back entrance of the parking garage."

He followed her to the metal staircase. Rachel scurried up the first flight of stairs ahead of him, then stumbled on the landing. He grabbed her elbow, trying to balance her as she reached down to adjust her shoe.

"You okay?" he asked.

"Yes, but next time I'm chased by bad guys, heels aren't the shoe of choice. I can't even feel my toes anymore."

"We could—"

"It's fine." She held up her hand, waving off any advice. "I just need to make it to your car."

She stopped again on the next landing. "This opens to a hallway. To the right is the fire door that leads outside."

Two more doors and they were outside where the dropping temperature would soon turn the light rain into ice. He glanced at her shivering figure. In their haste, she must have left her coat behind.

Aiden pulled off his jacket and handed it to her. "You're shaking."

"More from terror than the cold."

He helped her pull the tweed jacket close around her with his free hand, not waiting for another one of her excuses, then paused when she looked up at him. Her upper lip quivered. He could read the fear in her eyes, but there was also a note of determination. Why did she have to be so beautiful? Why did he have to notice?

He turned away abruptly. "Which way to the garage?"

"This way."

He followed her down the sidewalk toward the parking garage at the back of the connecting building, while placing another call to Shepherd. No answer. Frustration loomed again. He needed to talk to Shepherd. Needed his boss's help with an exit strategy.

Rachel stopped at another door and swiped her access card again in order to get inside the parking garage.

"This place is like Fort Knox," he said as the light turned green. "How did that guy manage to get into the lab?"

"He has to have an inside connection. It's the only way."

But who? The same person who had been hacking his communications from the field? There had to be more than one person behind this. Shepherd had told him not to trust anyone, but he needed to know more. The garage was quiet. It was late enough that only a couple of parked cars remained, including his rental.

The elevator on the far side dinged and someone emerged.

"Hold on." He grabbed her hand and pulled her back behind one of the cement columns as two men stepped out. He caught the profile of their Mr. X and felt his stomach churn. They were trapped. If they moved back toward the door where they'd entered the garage, they'd be seen. At the moment, there was no way to get to the car.

"We need to call 911," Rachel whispered.

"They won't get here in time, and besides, we'd lose the virus, and we can't afford that. We both know what will happen if it gets into the wrong hands."

"So what are our options?" she asked.

"There's a metro stop a couple of blocks from here, isn't there?"

"Two blocks away."

He glanced down at her feet. "And your shoes?"

"I'll be fine."

He peeked around the column. The men were having a heated conversation near his vehicle. If they started searching the garage, he and Rachel would be found before they could get to the car. Leaving by foot seemed like their best option.

"I say we take a chance and get out of here," she said.

Aiden nodded, then grabbed Rachel's hand. His foot kicked against a rock as he sped toward the door, and it ricocheted against the wall. So much for their stealthy exodus. One of the men shouted at them, but they kept running. Rachel managed to match his steps as they raced toward the door. A shot rang out, the bullet missing them by inches as it slammed into the cement wall next to them.

Outside the garage there was a side street leading to a string of restaurants, most of which had already closed for the night. The men were yelling again, but it was obvious they weren't sure which direction their prey had gone.

Aiden pulled Rachel behind a dumpster and crouched next to her. With any luck, they'd lost them. She leaned against him in the darkness. He could feel her pulse pounding against his hold on her wrist as she tried to catch her breath. His other hand gripped the handle of the insulated cooler box. For the first time in his life, he felt pulled between two very important choices. He'd been deployed over a dozen times through the rapid response medical team he worked with. His team had been assigned to outbreaks of pneumonic plague, cerebral meningitis, and a long list of other diseases, always aware of the risks involved. He'd worked in dangerous conditions alongside infection prevention control specialists and his own emergency medical response team. But he'd never been shot at, or chased by armed men, or had such an intense desire to protect a woman he'd just met.

The voices faded, but he hesitated to move for another few seconds. "I think we've lost them for the moment."

"The metro's not far."

He followed her down the side street, making sure they stayed in the shadows so they weren't caught in the light from the streetlamps.

"We're almost there." She was breathing hard as she tugged something out of her purse then handed it to him. "I always carry an extra metro card for when my brother comes to visit. You're going to need one."

He caught sight of a large post with an *M* marking the station then followed her down the escalator, his adrenaline still pumping. This late at night the loading platform was fairly empty, making it impossible to disappear into a crowd. But it also meant that whoever was after them couldn't hide either. He scanned the passengers as they got off the escalator, but there was no sign of either of the men who'd been after them. Lights flashed along the platform as the train approached. Seconds later, they stepped on the subway.

"Do you think they're still following us?" she asked, stumbling into one of the seats facing the doors where they could watch anyone coming in or out.

"I think we shook them." He caught her gaze. "You okay?"

"No, I'm not." Rachel leaned against the back of the seat and closed her eyes for a few seconds. "Apparently, you were right. Someone is willing to kill for a super virus with the potential to cause a worldwide pandemic. Your boss warned you not to trust anyone, my boss is missing, and on top of that, my heel just snapped off."

Aiden looked down at her shoes. The sling-back pumps couldn't be comfortable in a normal setting, and she'd somehow managed to run from a couple of bad guys in them in the middle of winter.

She tugged on the bottom of his jacket. "I'm sorry I'm having a meltdown, but I'm not going to apologize for freaking out. Not after everything that's happened today."

"I'm not asking you to." He held out his hand. "Give me the good shoe."

"Why?"

"Unless you want me to carry you off the metro and up the escalator when we reach our stop, I need you to be able to walk out of here on your own."

She frowned but handed him the shoe.

A second later, he'd popped off the heel, giving her a matching set of broken shoes. "Saw that in a movie."

"These heels weren't exactly cheap."

"I'll buy you a new pair."

"On a researcher's salary?" Her frown only deepened as he tried to read her expression. "Forget it."

"You're mad."

"Yeah, I am mad, though not about the shoe, and not at you." She rubbed the back of her neck, still frowning. "I'm used to dealing with tense situations in the lab. Deadly pathogens barely faze me. I respect them, and I'm careful, but they don't send me spiraling out of control. All of this. I don't like getting shot at. It reminds me of. . ."

"Of what?"

"It doesn't matter," she said, but from the sadness he saw flash across her face, there was more to her story. She was as complicated as any chemical formula and just as intriguing. "I just don't like bad guys chasing after me."

"Or not knowing who to trust."

"Exactly."

"We're going to figure this out."

"How?" She shivered and pulled his jacket tighter around herself. "How did a routine testing of a virus turn into me breaking my rules that never should have been broken?"

"The only thing that makes sense is that whoever hacked into my digital transactions is after the virus."

"But who is it?"

"I have no idea. Only a couple people knew I'd returned to the States. But with our online security compromised, I have no idea who knows what we're dealing with at this point."

She rested her hand on top of the insulated box sitting between them. "What do we do?"

"Not *we*. Me. I need to get you somewhere safe," Aiden said, making a decision. Dr. Moreno might have dragged her into this, but this wasn't her fight. And he wasn't going to let anything happen to her.

"Somewhere safe? Where would that be?" She shook her head. "We're not supposed to trust anyone, but we also can't keep running with this virus in our possession. Maintaining its integrity is essential if we're going to find a way to stop this pathogen from spreading."

They needed a plan. "We'll go back to my hotel. No one knows where I'm staying, so it will give you a safe place for now. Then, I don't know. I'll make some phone calls. See if I can get in touch with Shepherd. Track down your boss—"

"Aiden. . ."

"I see him."

The metro was pulling into another station. A man wearing black stood on the platform, same height and build as the man who'd shot at them. He was waiting for the train doors to open. The men couldn't have tracked them here, or could they? His phone was just a cheap burner phone, but Rachel had a smart phone.

"We need to get off," he said as the man stepped onto the metro. "Stay close."

He grabbed her hand but didn't move. Timing it so they were stepping off the metro a second before the doors slid shut behind them, so whoever was after them—if they really were after them—couldn't follow.

"You think that was one of them?" she asked as they hurried toward the escalator and up toward the street level.

"I don't know."

Shaking with outrage, Rachel stepped into the freezing night and yanked out her phone.

"What are you doing?" Aiden asked.

"Calling the police."

"No." He took her phone, smashed it under his boot, then threw it in the trash can on the curb.

"Hey!" She lunged for the trash can, but he snagged her arm.

"Maybe we're both overreacting, but if they tracked us to the subway, then that means they're tracking your phone."

"How do they even know who I am?"

"I don't know."

"So what do you propose we do?"

"I need to talk to Shepherd. He's got to have answers."

"And if he doesn't?"

Aiden ignored her question, refusing to consider that possibility. Instead, he surveyed the street, trying to orient himself. They were still a couple miles from his hotel, and on top of that, the rain had turned into a sleety mix. They needed to get off the street and out of the cold. The lights of an open café caught his attention.

"When's the last time you ate?" he asked.

"I don't remember. Why?"

"We need to get out of sight until we have some answers. Come with me."

SIX

Sleet pellets pounded the windows of the diner Aiden had dragged her into. At least rain on the windows of the small café created a protective curtain between them and the bad guys. But Rachel felt like they were sitting ducks in a carnival booth. Easily picked off by the men with guns. Guys with no more qualms against doing harm than the drug lord who'd gunned down her father. And now, she and Aiden had foolishly allowed these evil men to chase them into a corner. Bad guys who'd do anything to get the virus.

Heart still pounding, Rachel twisted the hem of her dress and watched water puddle on the black and white tiles of the diner floor.

"Is your dress ruined?" he asked.

"Probably," eeked from between her chattering teeth.

"Send me the bill." He pointed at her mangled shoes. "For the heels and the phone too."

"Forget it. Those are the least of my worries right now."

"I know you're afraid, but once I can hook back up with my team, everything's going to be okay."

"You don't know that." She realized from the edge in her voice that she was more angry than afraid. Very angry. But mad as she was at the man who'd just dumped her phone into the trash, she was even angrier at herself for trusting him. Memories she'd fought to erase over the past decade surfaced. She'd heard gunfire coming from the river. She'd disobeyed her parents' rules and left their cinderblock house in the Amazon jungle. The tragedy she'd witnessed when she peered through the foliage had changed her life, and that painful image had taught her to never make another move without thinking through every possible consequence of breaking the rules. She'd learned to value predictability and the security that came from knowing what was going to happen next.

Her brother, on the other hand, had witnessed the same event, but his reaction had been totally the opposite. Watching their father die had made Josiah impulsive and reckless. If Josiah were here right now, he'd howl at the improbability of his little sister being so easily convinced by a man, especially a man she'd just met, to steal a deadly virus, and then recklessly trust said stranger to help her evade men with guns.

And Josiah would be right. She knew the possible dangers this virus possessed, and Aiden Ballinger was as unpredictable as the virus she'd stupidly let him talk her into removing from the safety of a Level 4 containment lab. She could claim she'd fallen prey to his charms, but what she wanted to do was kick herself with her broken shoes.

How can I fix this?

Aiden squeezed her hand, and Rachel startled from her thoughts. "Look," he said in a low, calming voice, "why don't you order us some coffee and something to eat, and I'll try to track down my team, okay?" He regarded her the way her mother used to when she wanted her to see her side of things, then he fished his phone from his pants pocket. "Black and strong for me."

"You're just going to sit down and drink a cup of coffee like nothing's happened?"

"Comes with the job."

"Maybe for a virus hunter, but nowhere in the lab-geek manual does it state that the average researcher should expect to be pursued by gunfire." Rachel fisted the jacket closed around her trembling body. "I chose a boring life because. . .it doesn't matter why."

"I think it does." He lifted the laminated menu out from behind the napkin holder. "Burger medium well. Lettuce and tomato only."

"Anything else, Captain America?"

"If I can't get Shepherd, maybe someone else on the team can help us out."

Rachel wanted to tell him she wasn't getting paid enough to take his dinner order let alone take a bullet on behalf of world safety, so she was going home, but a tall woman was blocking her exit from the booth.

"You two lovebirds ready to order?"

Matchstick thin, in her mid-fifties, and wearing cat-eye glasses and too much red lipstick, the server looked like she'd just stepped out of one of those thriller films where the hero and heroine duck into a restaurant to escape evil pursuers. Oh wait. That's exactly what they'd just done.

"We're not together. . .I mean. . .we're not lovebirds. . .I mean, yeah, I'll order for the both of us." Rachel's teeth had stopped chattering but her hair was still dripping onto the table. "Two black coffees. Hot. Two burgers." Rachel proceeded to repeat Aiden's burger specifications and when she realized they matched her own, a strange sensation buzzed in her stomach. "I'll have the same."

"That all?" the woman asked, pen hovering over her pad.

"When do you close?"

"About an hour." The server let her eyes crawl over Rachel's disheveled appearance. "You two expecting company?"

"No." Rachel's panicked response raised the penciled eyebrows of the woman.

"I've got an extra pair of sneakers that might fit you."

"Excuse me?"

"Saw you limping in your broken heels." She let her gaze slide to Rachel's feet. "Must have been some party."

"Yeah," Rachel said. "Real wild."

"Want the sneakers?"

She had to return to the lab and fix this somehow. She could call for an Uber ride. Should she even trust an Uber driver? If she had to take a bus or the subway, she'd have to walk, and the sleet was turning the streets and sidewalks into a skating rink.

"I'll pay you for them," Rachel said.

"Help someone else someday." The woman ripped their order sheet from the pad and slid her pen above her ear. "I'll get those sneakers right out to you and see that you and that cute boyfriend of yours get some extra fries."

Boyfriend?

Before Rachel could set the record straight again, the woman sashayed across the empty diner and shouted their order to the round-bellied man scraping the day's grease buildup from the grill behind the long counter.

Aiden snapped his flip phone shut. "Shepherd is still not answering, and now I can't get Iceman either."

"Our kind server is bringing me some shoes."

"What?"

"I can't go much farther in these." Rachel held up what was left of the heels Cara had talked her into. "Besides, if we didn't shake whoever was following us, I think they'd be here by now, don't you?" She would have laughed at sounding like a character from a thriller movie, but Aiden's sober face killed the thought. "What is it?"

"My team always answers my calls."

She leaned forward. "I still say we need to call the police."

"And tell them what? That we stole an ancient virus from a Level 4 lab and then the security guards chased us?"

"Well, when you put it that way." He could push all he wanted, but she wasn't making another move without thinking through every consequence.

Aiden shoved his phone in his pocket. "I haven't eaten all day, and if this is going to be my last meal, I plan to enjoy it."

Last meal? She assumed he was joking, but instead of reinforcing her lack of a sense of humor, she said, "Tell me about this Iceman."

"My freshman year of college, Calum Lewis waltzed into our dorm room like he owned the joint, threw his rucksack on the empty bunk, then stuck out his hand in an offer of friendship." Aiden rubbed his chin. "We've had each other's back ever since."

"Have you tried calling his family? Maybe they've heard from him."

"His mother's dead and he hasn't seen his father since third grade."

"How could he afford Columbia?"

"You really have stalked me."

"Maybe, but there's still clearly a lot I don't know about you."

The server showed up with two hot coffees, two burgers, extra fries, and a pair of size seven sneakers as promised. "Eat up, kids."

Rachel thanked the beaming woman for the shoes, then slipped them on. "I don't know anything about your family, other than that you grew up in Philadelphia. I'm sure your parents would want to know if you're in danger."

He chewed slowly then swallowed. "Probably. What about you? Anyone we need to alert on your behalf? A boyfriend? Husband? Parents?"

"No boyfriend or husband." She'd survived the loss of her father, and after her mother remarried, it had felt like she'd lost her too. She'd learned to be a survivor. "My mom and I don't keep up that well, but I have an older brother who lives in California that I'm pretty close to."

"Maybe you should go there."

"Josiah has a busy surgery practice, a wife and my niece Emma that I would not want to put in danger."

They ate in silence for a few moments while Aiden polished off his burger. "I think you're right."

"About?"

"Letting my parents know what's going on. My dad has connections and will be able to help us both. It would give us time to figure out what's going on, and we'd be able to keep the virus safe."

"We?"

"Sure. I don't know why I didn't think of this before."

"You want me to go to your parents'?" Rachel shook her head. "If I don't show up at work tomorrow, people will think I had something to do with all of this."

"You know as well as I that it's not safe to go back to the lab, Rachel."

"If we return the vials, show the higher-ups what we saw on the security feed, they'll see that we had no choice but to take the samples and run." She bent over and tied her new sneakers. "I may get in some trouble for giving you access to the lab, but once we tell them about the blood in Dr. Moreno's office, they'll understand—"

"I think this is way bigger than us simply throwing out an explanation. I'm more concerned that they'd confiscate the virus while trying to sort everything out. And that can't happen. If you won't go to my parents', at least let me get you a room next to mine at the hotel. I'll sleep better knowing you're safe."

She frowned at the plan. "I'm not sure sleep is going to be possible."

"How far do you live from here?" Aiden asked, ignoring the comment.

"Just a few blocks."

"Okay, we'll swing by your place and get you some dry clothes. You can call your brother on my phone and warn him about what's going on, but then you're coming with me. We'll work together to make sure you keep your job, and even more importantly, that we both keep our lives, okay?"

Rachel considered his arguments and weighed them against everything that had transpired since she'd come in contact with the vials tucked inside the cooler sitting beside the attractive and convincing virus hunter. As much as she loved predictability, she knew living pathogens could not be trusted to play by the rules. Sometimes they tried to stump you by refusing to give up their secrets. Or sometimes they tried to trip you up with false positives. And sometimes the unsolved mysteries of a virus were like the unsolved mysteries of life. . .They could only be solved by stepping out of the bounds of safety.

Her gaze latched onto Aiden's. She was already in over her head. And as far as she was concerned, they were out of options.

Then and there she made another impulsive decision. "I'll go with you."

"Good." He pulled out a couple twenties and set them on the table. "Because we have less than seventy-two hours before the virus begins to decompensate."

SEVEN

Aiden slid in next to Rachel in the back seat of the Uber. While he might need her expertise with viruses at some point, having her with him did complicate the situation. But it had been his own string of decisions that had led to her involvement. Which made him feel responsible. And now, without any idea who they could trust, keeping her with him seemed like the only way to ensure her safety.

He glanced out the window as their driver merged into traffic that was still heavy this time of night. He'd been paranoid after learning about the security breach in their system while in Tibet. So paranoid, in fact, that he'd not only bought a burner phone that couldn't be traced, but he'd used a fake name when checking into his DC hotel. At the time, he'd felt as if he were overreacting. Now he knew he hadn't been. The one thing he'd done right was to secure a place off the radar where they could hole up until they knew what was going on. But every minute spent protecting their own hides decreased their chances of saving countless lives. Time was not on their side.

"We're going to figure this out," he said, hoping the lilt in his voice made up for his lack of confidence in the situation.

"Maybe, but in order to figure it out, we need to know who's behind your security breach," she said. "Dr. Moreno was very insistent that we not leave a digital trail." She pulled the little notebook from her purse. "None of what I learned about the rapid replication abilities of this virus is on a computer."

"Unless my hacker also works inside Gaumond. What about Cara?"

"Cara? You know her as well as I do. She's harmless, and besides, I didn't tell her what I was doing. I can't imagine her being involved in something like this."

Which led to another set of questions. If whoever was after them had tracked Rachel's phone, which they must have done to find them on the subway, how had they figured out Rachel was involved in the first place? There was no way to know at this point, which only added to his uneasiness. He needed to get her somewhere safe.

His phone rang and he pulled it out of his pocket, hoping for some good news.

"Who is it?" she asked.

Aiden glanced at the caller ID.

"Veronica Waybright. She's a clinical research nurse and works part time as Shepherd's assistant." He answered the call. "Veronica, I've been trying to contact Shepherd for hours. I've left him messages. I've left you messages. What's going on?"

Rachel leaned in close so she could listen.

There was a pause on the line before Veronica responded. "I don't know how to say this, Aiden, but Nate's dead."

"Wait a minute. What?" He lowered the volume on his phone so their driver couldn't overhear. "How?"

"I'm not sure anyone knows yet. I'm here now with the police and his wife. Apparently, his car went into the C&O Canal near Chain Bridge Road. There was alcohol in the car."

Aiden shook his head as he tried to take in the news. The strongest drink he'd ever seen his boss order was a double shot of espresso. Never alcohol.

"Shepherd doesn't drink," Aiden said. "He's been sober for over a decade."

"That's what his wife told the authorities. They're going to do an autopsy, but until then that's all I can tell you. I'm sorry."

"So am I. Keep me updated."

A sick feeling washed through Aiden as he hung up the phone.

Rachel turned to him. "I'm sorry, Aiden. I don't know what to say."

"I don't either." He dropped the phone into his lap then rubbed the back of his neck in an attempt to wake from this horrible nightmare.

She leaned forward. Her words barely a whisper. "We aren't the only ones they're willing to kill to find this virus, are we?"

He caught fear in her voice. Shepherd's death couldn't be filed away as a coincidence. He'd asked the man to look into the security breaches in order to find out who was behind them. So what had happened? Had Shepherd asked one too many questions? Gotten too close to the person who knew the truth? Clearly he'd discovered something, but what? Or had someone just decided to make sure he didn't dig any deeper?

Rachel's fingers squeezed his arm. "Your boss is dead. Mine is missing. Whoever wants this virus is not going to stop looking until they find us."

He laid his hand on hers, not sure how to respond. Her breathing was accelerated, and her face had blanched white. "Are you okay?"

"I'll be fine." She turned away from him and stared out the window as their car sped through the wet streets and rain pinged against the windows.

"You're shaking." He wrapped his arm around her shoulder and drew her close.

Her gaze met his. "My father was murdered when I was a kid."

"Oh. Wow. . ." Her confession took him off guard. "I'm so sorry."

"I was young and don't remember him as much as my brother, but this. . ," She waved her hand in the air. "It triggered something deep inside of me, and I'm there again in my mind. Watching my mother cry on the long flight back to Kansas. People filling my grandparents' fridge with casseroles and Jell-O. Not really understanding what was happening, but realizing on one level that life would never be the same again."

Aiden studied her tear-streaked face, wanting to help, but not wanting to pry. "What else can you tell me about it?"

"My father was a doctor who felt called to help the indigenous people of Columbia. My brother and I grew up on the banks of the Amazon River. One day my father tried to help the wrong people. They killed him. Just like your boss. . .maybe Moreno. . .all because of someone's greed."

Normally, he would have enjoyed the lights of the city, but tonight he barely noticed. He didn't know how in only a few hours something had connected between them, but it had. And now his heart unexpectedly broke for her.

"I'm sorry. Truly sorry."

She shrugged. "We came back to the States and life went on, but I still think about him."

Their driver pulled to a stop in front of a red brick townhouse. Aiden asked the man to wait for them, then hurried up the stairs behind Rachel to her apartment.

She pulled out her key, then stopped. "Aiden. . ."

"What's wrong?"

She pushed the door open with her foot. "Someone's been inside."

Aiden stepped into the doorway then glanced into the living room. "Wait here."

"I'm coming with you." She grabbed his arm and followed him through the open living room and kitchen area, then to the adjoining bedroom and bathroom. On any other day he would have enjoyed seeing where she lived. Photos of the Amazon jungle hung on the wall next to a picture of her as a little girl with her family, but there was no time to study them.

Whoever had been here was long gone, but his apprehension had just multiplied exponentially.

"Can you tell if anything was taken?"

"I'm not sure." She turned slowly in the ransacked living room. "I'm trying hard not to freak out. I only heard about this virus today. If they got to Dr. Moreno and he told them I'd been working on it. . ."

Her theory made sense. And it answered the question he'd asked himself earlier. There was no doubt now that someone believed Rachel was key to whatever they had planned for the virus.

"We need to get out of here," he said. "I want you to grab some clothes for a couple days and your passport. You do have a passport, right?"

"Of course." She turned and faced him. "But why would I need a passport?"

"We need to keep our options open."

A plan had started to form in his mind, but if he told her, he was worried she'd balk. It had been weeks since he and his father had spoken, and their last encounter had ended in a fight. As an only child, he'd never lived up to his father's expectations of taking on the family business, but right now it didn't matter that his plans didn't fit with his father's. Not today.

"Rachel?"

She'd picked up a shattered frame off the floor and held it against her. "It's the last photo I have of my father and me. Why did they go through my stuff? Did they think I'd hide a deadly virus beneath the sofa cushions?"

"Rachel—"

Her gaze shifted, and the color drained from her face. She bent and picked up another photo. It appeared as if someone had ripped away whoever had been standing beside a grown-up Rachel on the beach. "They know about my brother and his family."

He nodded, the decision made. Like it or not, there was only one option.

"I know who can help us." He glanced at the door. "Let's go."

EIGHT

Rachel stepped out into the freezing night then glanced back at her townhouse one last time. For the sake of her brother and his family, she had no choice but to trust this man she'd met only a couple of hours ago. She threw her small carry-on into the back seat then blindly climbed inside. Aiden crowded in next to her, his close proximity strangely comforting despite her reluctance to continue with him and his dangerous quest to protect this deadly virus. She'd never forgive herself if her foolish professional crush on a virus hunter brought harm to her brother and his family.

Aiden ignored the driver's question as to where they wanted to go. Instead, he told the man he'd dole out verbal directions as they went along, directions that he wanted followed to a *T*. They stayed off the main thoroughfares and zipped down side streets and alleys like they were in some kind of movie chase scene.

Thirty minutes later, and with more questions than answers tumbling about in her frantic thoughts, Rachel heard Aiden instruct their driver to let them out under the sail-shaped porte cochère of the Watergate Hotel. The iconic building, which had been closed for over a decade, had undergone a major renovation. Modern lights artfully lit up the home of the 1970s scandal that had brought down a president.

"We're going to get help here?" she asked.

"This is where I'm staying."

"This is quite a hotel." She dragged her suitcase with its missing wheel across the gleaming black floors of the lobby, feeling suddenly out of place.

"I was going more for discretion than location when I booked."

Rachel had considered taking a tour of this hotel when it first reopened. She'd read that the scandal room from the 1972 political break-in had been redecorated with Nixon-era memorabilia, including a manual typewriter and a reel-to-reel tape recorder. She was pondering how often and why Aiden came to DC when one of the two men behind the expansive concierge's desk looked up.

He smiled as if he recognized Aiden and said, "Good evening, Mr. Darlington."

Aiden tucked the cooler under his arm. "Anyone ask for me, Romano?"

"Not on my shift, sir," Romano said.

Aiden took Rachel's elbow and hurried her to the elevator. "Let's hope we're still a step ahead of whoever wants this virus."

The elevator doors opened and they stepped inside. "Mr. Darlington?"

Aiden shrugged. "I was paranoid when I got here and didn't want anyone to be able to track me down. Now I'm glad I was."

"Is that the reason for the flip phone as well?"

"Yep."

"I work with dangerous viruses every day, but I've never had a need to change my name."

"If it keeps us safe. . ."

The elevator dinged and Aiden stepped into a quiet hallway of the top floor. Rachel hesitated. Who was this man? Since she'd met him, she'd found blood in her boss's office, she'd been chased and shot at, her phone had been destroyed, her home ransacked, and now her brother's life could be threatened. If she followed Aiden to one of the suites and there was more trouble, she couldn't even phone for help. Which is what she should have done back at Dr. Moreno's office. But if she backed out now, she would be on her own and she wouldn't know how to begin to secure her brother's safety.

Aiden signaled for her to stop in front of the *Do Not Disturb* sign. "Better stand back."

He slid his electronic key into the lock and cautiously pushed the door open. He stepped into the dark room and ambient lighting came on. Lavish finishes and sleek furniture filled the one-bedroom executive suite, but the thing that caught Rachel's eye was the floor-to-ceiling windows and the sweeping view of the Potomac River.

"No one's been in here," he said, sounding relieved.

"I'm turning on the TV to see if there's any news from the lab." Rachel clicked the remote, and a breaking news story about a body discovered in a research lab parking garage flashed on the huge flat screen. No name was mentioned, but the sick feeling in her gut confirmed the fears growing faster than the virus in monkey cells.

"Aiden. . .It has to be Moreno." She sat down on the end of the bed, her hands trembling as she set the remote down next to her. Nate Shepherd had ended up in a canal, and now they'd gotten to Moreno? How long before they found them?

Aiden sat down next to her as a woman reported the story from outside the lab with nothing more than a handful of sketchy details.

We need answers, God. We need to know who's behind this.

"We should call Dr. Moreno's wife," she said. "Find out what she knows."

Aiden shook his head. "We can't take a chance of whoever's behind this tracing us through her phone, and I don't want to risk putting her life in any more danger. If it's him, she'll be there with the authorities."

Aiden went to a built-in cabinet, opened the door, and punched in the code on the in-room safe. She watched as he pulled out a wad of cash and two passports then picked up the house phone. He dialed a number and told the person on the other end to have the plane ready.

"A plane?" Rachel whispered.

"I booked a charter."

"A charter?" Rachel stammered as dollar signs whirled in her head. "How much will that cost?"

"We're covered."

"By whom?"

"You have just enough time to change into something dry and call your family," he said, ignoring her question. "We leave from Reagan International in an hour. It's less than fifteen minutes from here, so that should give us time to get through security," he said, ignoring her question.

"Where are we going?"

"To the one man who can help us sort this out." Aiden threw his personal items into a backpack, stuffed the money and passports in a side pocket, then grabbed the cooler. "Let's go."

An hour later, they were the only two passengers buckled into the plush leather seats of a private jet. "We'll change planes in Miami," Aiden told her once they were airborne.

"Wait a minute. . ." She shifted toward him in her seat. "Where do your parents live?"

"It's out of the country."

She unclicked her seat belt, feeling the panic returning. "We're leaving the country?"

"Rachel, sit down. Please."

"Are they expecting us?"

He nodded. "I sent a message."

She looked around the cabin. Outside the window, the lights of DC were tiny dots. Since she didn't have a parachute, she had no choice but to drop back into her seat. "When you said your parents could help, I was thinking we were going to some house in the suburbs, or downtown loft, but out of the US?"

"It's the safest thing for now." He poured her a cup of the hot tea he'd ordered from the only flight attendant on the plane. "My mom will be happy I've finally brought a girl home." He smiled and handed her the cup.

If he was trying to lighten the mood and convince her to release her death grip on the armrests, his approach wasn't working. "Where, exactly, do your parents live?"

"It's a remote location. Drink."

Rachel took the mug. The floral-scented concoction enticed her to take a long sip. "Someone needs to know what happened to us tonight. What could happen if we don't handle this right."

"Look, I know this all seems crazy, but you're going to have to trust me." Aiden undid his seat belt. He stood and retrieved a pillow and a blanket from a tiny closet. "Try to get some rest. We'll figure this out. Okay?"

Rachel took the bedding, not because she enjoyed being told what to do, but because her ebbing adrenaline was already giving way to the sheer exhaustion pressing down on her. And being wrapped in a blanket seemed like it would somehow make her feel less exposed. Besides, she needed clear-headed thinking to untangle the mess she'd made when she allowed a stranger, no matter how charming, access to a secret, high-level biocontainment research lab. Even more foolish was the undeniable fact that she'd let this same man talk her out of calling the police when they found blood in Dr. Moreno's office. Whether or not she could be considered an accomplice to tonight's long list of questionable activities was nothing compared to agreeing to follow a man she knew only from his social media posts aboard a sleek jet bound for who knew where. Truth was, foolish as all of this sounded, she had no other way to satisfy her insatiable need to know everything about the deadly virus in those vials. When it came to the need-to-know-department, it was apparent that she and the man sitting in the seat opposite her and rubbing his stubbled face were a lot alike.

"Aiden, the viability clock is ticking on that virus."

He gave her an appreciative half grin. "My father's an expert when it comes to beating the clock."

"Who are you?"

"Close your eyes," he said. "I'll wake you when we land in Miami."

It was still dark when Rachel dragged her broken bag across the steamy Florida tarmac and boarded another private plane.

"Where's the pilot?"

Aiden flashed her a smile. "You're looking at him." He climbed into the pilot seat. "You're welcome to ride shotgun, or you can stretch out in the back."

"Do you walk on water too?" Rachel slipped into the co-pilot seat and frowned. Surely there was something the man couldn't do. "I'm not taking a back seat again." She adjusted the earphones on her head.

Soon they were high above the Atlantic and hurtling toward a rosy glow in the southeastern sky.

Aiden navigated with the skill of a military pilot, pointing out points of interest in the dark water below. "It's going to be a couple of hours before we get there. You might want to try to get some more sleep before you have to face my dad."

She could add another hundred questions to her growing list. Was this his plane? Where were they going? Why should she be worried about meeting his father? But her need to have all the information neatly categorized and under her control quickly gave way to sheer exhaustion.

She woke to a gentle elbow nudge.

Aiden was staring at her. "Hey." He'd been up most of the night, but he didn't seem the least bit weary.

Rachel sat up and straightened her earphones. "Hi." Her dry-throat croak into the headset mic generated a smile on Aiden's stubbled face.

"You talk in your sleep."

"What did I say?"

"Something about jungles and rivers."

Rachel turned her head and pressed her nose to the glass, watching as the plane swept low over azure waters so clear she could see a tinge of pink on the sandy ocean floor. Her nightmares didn't often slip through the wall she'd built around the memories of that long-ago day, but they were her business. Not his. "Where are we?"

"A private island off Bermuda."

A familiar panic welled in Rachel's empty stomach. "People go into the Bermuda Triangle and never come out."

"Relax." He slicked his tousled hair back. "My family's been flying in and out of here my whole life."

The plane circled a small compound situated on a projection of land covered in lush vegetation. Several small, white, tin-roofed buildings spooled off a larger main house. A private dock led to the water where a large yacht-like boat was tethered to the pier. The other side of the property sported an airstrip that did not appear long enough for this plane to safely land and a helipad. Rachel felt the jerk of the descending landing gear. She dug her fingers into the armrest and took a big breath. She didn't breathe again until the plane taxied to a stop beside a waiting golf cart and a man with a face as weathered as driftwood.

"Come on." Aiden unclicked his seat belt. "Benny is getting too old to sit out in the heat."

"Who's Benny?"

"Benny's my parents' estate manager who has been working for my family as long as I can remember. He takes care of everything from security to privacy. You'll love him." Aiden climbed out of his seat. "Plus, we need to get this virus on some fresh ice." He grabbed the transport cooler he'd stowed in a tiny closet then pressed a button that opened the jet door.

"What about our bags?"

"I don't think you're going to need those sweaters you packed right away." He offered her his hand. "Don't worry, Mom is used to getting visitors all fixed up."

"But my passport and—"

"It'll be safe. Come on. The clock's ticking."

He didn't need to remind her of the shelf-life of a virus or the possible threat to her brother. They needed to talk about what was going on and what they should do ASAP. Rachel gathered her scattered thoughts and fears and followed after him.

Salt, sea, and surf perfumed the tropical breeze. She thought she knew everything there was to know about Aiden Ballinger. But perhaps if she'd studied him with the same intensity that she studied viruses she might have known he had his secrets.

NINE

Aiden stepped off the plane and onto the asphalt runway, trying not to second-guess his decision to bring Rachel to the island. When they'd left DC, his parents' vacation home on the isolated island had seemed like the one place he could keep her safe. Now that they were here, he wasn't sure his rash decision to fly her had been the right one. Banking on his father's help was never certain.

"Wow." Rachel stopped in front of him, shifting his attention momentarily back to her. "I can see why your family loves it here. White beaches, blue waters as far as you can see. . .This place is stunning."

"You can see the entire island from Cook's Peak," he said, nodding toward the north of them.

She brushed back a strand of hair the wind had blown across her face. "Who owns this place?"

Aiden hesitated. "It belongs to my family."

"Wait. . ." Her eyes widened at the admission. "Your family owns this whole island?"

He shrugged, not sure if she was impressed by the revelation or if it would make her even more cynical toward him. "It's not exactly something I talk about on my YouTube channel. In fact, I've worked hard to keep this part of me off the Internet."

"I'll say. You have a lot of explaining to do."

"I'll tell you everything as soon as we get settled. I promise. Trust me."

The look on her face made it clear that she still didn't completely trust him. Not that he blamed her. But this wasn't the world he lived in most of the time. In fact, this was the world he'd tried to leave. And ironically, it was now the one place he hoped he could keep her safe. There was no time to explain further as Benny ushered them onto the golf cart.

"Welcome to Jade Island," the older man said, with a grin.

"It's great to see you, Benny." Aiden quickly made introductions. "How are you?"

"Things are well here, though probably not as exciting as where you've been. I heard you went to Tibet to wrangle a virus."

"I was there, and. . ." Aiden handed him a sealed, foil package he'd brought with him. "I brought you back some coffee beans from the Himalayans."

The older man shot him an affectionate smile. "Aiden always brings me something from his trips, and knows I'm a bit of a coffee connoisseur."

"Just a bit of a connoisseur?" Aiden laughed as he turned to Rachel. "To Benny, coffee is more than just a drink, it's an experience."

"You know me well."

Which was true, but Aiden didn't miss the disturbing signs as they headed toward the house, that Benny had aged since he'd last seen him. The lines around his eyes and mouth had deepened and his graying hair was now white at his temples and goatee. Maybe he'd simply taken for granted the idea that Benny would be with them forever.

His mother and father were waiting for them in front of the Caribbean-styled villa that offered dramatic views of the sea and equally striking sunsets.

"You didn't give us much time to prepare," his mother said, pulling him into a hug while the wind tugged at the hem of her white maxi dress. "It's good to see you."

"You always like surprises, and it was a. . .a spur of the moment decision." Aiden glanced briefly at Rachel. "I figured you wouldn't mind."

"We've been trying to get you to bring a girl here for years." His mother's expectant gaze demanded an explanation and an introduction of the girl he'd dragged into this mess.

Aiden took a step back and gently grasped Rachel's elbow. "I want you to meet Dr. Rachel Allen. Rachel, this is my mom and dad, Grant and Iris Ballinger."

"It's good to meet you." His father's eyes brightened as he shook her hand. "You've been holding back on us, Son. I'm surprised we haven't heard about you, Rachel. How did you meet?"

Aiden glanced at Rachel. "At a fundraiser in DC."

Aiden scrambled for a better explanation, but Rachel beat him to it. "I've been following your son's career for several years now. So when we actually met, I felt as if I already knew him."

"I'm surprised that someone as young and clearly charming as yourself would be following the career of a virus hunter," his father said. "It can't be all that interesting to you."

"On the contrary," Rachel said. "I've always found the viral world fascinating."

"Rachel's a researcher in the same field," Aiden said, "and very good at what she does."

"We'll have time to get to know each other, I'm sure." His mother waved them past the pool and toward the house. "In the meantime, breakfast is almost ready."

Aiden caught the fatigue in his mother's eyes and hesitated. "Are you feeling okay, Mom?"

"A bit tired, but I'm fine. The down time here on the island has been a welcome relief after the non-stop pace back in the US."

"Good. I'd like to talk to Dad for a few minutes before we eat, if that's okay. Would you mind helping Rachel get settled and maybe give her a tour of the house? And she's not exactly prepared for the warmer temperatures."

His mother's brow rose. "Of course. Grab some coffee. It's hot. I'll take care of her."

"We won't be long," Aiden said, avoiding Rachel's glare. Clearly, she wasn't happy about being left alone with his mother.

He swallowed the guilt and followed his parents into the spacious house with its bamboo floors, boho décor, and his mom's collection of floral prints and colored glass pieces, trying to see the familiar space through Rachel's eyes. He and his dad grabbed mugs of coffee in the open kitchen after he placed the cooler in the freezer, then headed to his father's office. Like the rest of the house, the room had floor-to-ceiling windows overlooking stunning views of the water.

His father walked to his credenza. "Care for a shot of Irish whiskey in your coffee?"

Aiden held up his hand. "Black is fine. Thanks."

"It's been quite a while since we've seen you," his father said, adding a splash to his own cup. "Though I have to say, I'm surprised you brought someone so beautiful and accomplished with you."

He took a sip of his coffee. "Rachel and I are just. . .friends."

"Flying all the way here to meet your parents doesn't seem to imply simply friends."

"In this situation it does."

"And what situation would that be?"

Aiden moved toward the large window overlooking the ocean, trying to remember the speech he'd memorized on the way over. "You know I just returned from Tibet."

"I knew you were called to work there with the response team."

Aiden heard the disapproval in his father's voice. He'd made it clear that while Rapid Response Teams might be a noble pursuit, it didn't fit in with the overarching goals of the company or his plans for his son. Any arguments Aiden had countered with had been quickly shot down. Rumor had it that Tibet was going to be the last time the team was sent out.

"We've run into a few issues," Aiden admitted.

"Which is exactly why I've always said you can have far more impact running Gaumond Technology than you ever could chasing down viruses. You need to be at the helm of everything we do, not hidden in some remote location."

"You know I'd never be happy in a suit and tie. I'd never fit in."

"I don't know why you insist on holding that stance. The benefits would far outweigh any disadvantages. Your mother and I spend weeks here every year. We can go anywhere we want to go, buy anything we want to buy. It's the life we want for you."

"But is this really enough?"

"Enough? How could this not be enough?" His father waved his hand toward the view. "How can you not want all of this?"

Aiden tugged at the worn bracelet on his wrist. He hadn't come here to fight with his father, and he'd best remember that if he was going to secure the virus and the safety of Rachel's family.

"I'm not saying that what goes on in the field isn't important," his father continued. "But anyone can do that. I've been grooming you for years to take over the company. I think you're missing the point. What we do makes a difference."

Aiden swallowed the bitter words threatening to surface. "I'm grateful for your confidence in me, and I'll always be grateful to you for what you've taught me, but I've never been interested in the bottom line and the financial implications of running a business like this. Besides, there are plenty of other people who can run the company."

"But they're not my son."

Aiden blew out a frustrated breath. There was no use arguing. He'd never change his father's mind. But neither was he going to back down from what he believed was important.

"Tell me why you're really here," his father said.

Aiden shoved his hands into his pockets. "I need your help."

"I should have known."

"We discovered something unique behind a strange sickness in Tibet. Something I've never seen before."

"I've been keeping up on the daily reports. But I thought you'd pulled out of there?"

"Only temporarily. I took the virus to DC to have it retested."

His father took a sip of his drink. "What did you find?"

"Not only is the ancient virus viable, we confirmed that it is able to replicate in vertebrates."

"So a dormant giant virus has managed to infect humans, and it's spreading."

Aiden nodded. "But there's more at play here. For starters, there was a security breach in our communications."

His father's eyes darkened.

"And that's not all." Aiden hesitated before dropping the second bombshell. "Nate Shepherd is dead, and we think Moreno is as well."

His father set his drink down on his desk. "What?"

"Last night they found Shepherd's car in a canal in DC. They say he was drinking, but you and I both know he doesn't drink. On top of that, a body was found at the lab. I can't confirm it yet, but Rachel and I believe it was Moreno. There was blood in his office."

His father downed the rest of his drink then moved toward the window. "And you think this is all connected to the virus."

"You know as well as I do that the same technology we use to neutralize a virus can also turn it into a bioweapon. All they'd need is the perfect sample."

"And so you came here with the virus?"

"I came here to figure out what we need to do to stop this before more people get hurt."

His father stared out the window. "I know it's possible to reconstruct the virus, but there are a limited number of places and highly-trained personnel who could do this."

"You're right," Aiden said. "Which narrows down who might be behind it."

And added another option he hadn't considered before. What if they weren't just after the virus? In order to reconstruct a virus two things were needed: a high-tech lab and highly-trained personnel.

His father turned around. "Maybe you're overreacting. You don't conclusively know Nate Shepherd was murdered, do you?"

"I know Nate. He didn't drink and drive himself off a bridge."

"But you don't know that any more than you know that Moreno is actually dead."

"There was blood in his office." Aiden caught his father's gaze.

"Aiden—"

"There's more, Dad. We were shot at in the parking garage of the lab, then followed from there. Someone broke into Rachel's apartment. They took part of a photo of Rachel's family to send a message. The virus we have. . .Someone is willing to kill for it."

"Okay. Then what can I do?" On the surface, the question seemed helpful, but he couldn't allow the another-mess-of-yours-to-clean-up tone to derail him.

"I need a place that is safe for Rachel while I try to figure out what's going on. I was hoping you'd help. I thought you could help me brainstorm on what to do next."

"What are you thinking so far?"

"The obvious answer would be cloning it synthetically. That way there could be a broader scope of tests and drugs stopping the spread."

"On the surface I would agree, but this isn't going to be easy."

Aiden clasped his hands behind his back. "There's one person who could help us. He's off the grid and more than capable —"

"No," his father said. "Absolutely not."

Aiden could feel the frosty air slip between them, despite the warm temperature of the room. He'd once again pushed where he shouldn't have, but he didn't have a choice. They were way past playing it safe.

"It was never proven he was guilty," Aiden said.

"Or that he tampered with lab results, but we all know he did."

"Do we? You knew Charlie for years. He was your best friend. He mentored me —"

"What was I supposed to do? I protected him from legal consequences, but I couldn't keep him on at the company."

Aiden frowned. Rehashing what had happened wasn't going to change anything. "If not Charlie, then who? This is beyond either of us."

"I'll make a few discreet calls. See if I can come up with some answers."

"We don't have a lot of time," Aiden said, "and this has to stay under the radar. No one can know where the virus is."

His father's frown deepened, but he nodded. "I understand."

Aiden followed his father out of the office toward the dining room, hoping he hadn't made a mistake in coming here.

TEN

Rachel buttoned the jean shorts Mrs. Ballinger had delivered to her room, after insisting Aiden show his guest the beauty of their island in the moonlight.

If the Lord Himself had told her she would be wasting a day in a tropical paradise after stealing from her employer and running for her life, she wouldn't have believed it.

Since their arrival, she'd had breakfast overlooking the brilliant blue waters of the Atlantic. A long nap in a sumptuous king-sized bed with sheets softer than anything she'd ever experienced. And a three-hour golf cart tour of the grounds with Mrs. Ballinger at the wheel. Rachel had not seen Aiden again until dinner. If he was worried about the clock ticking on the viability of the virus, he didn't mention it once during the meal.

"You've not lived until you've had a midnight swim beneath a Bermuda moon," Mrs. Ballinger said as she bustled into Rachel's room after dinner and laid out a swimsuit, the shorts, and a sleeveless pink T-shirt.

"You really didn't have to go to all this trouble —"

"It'll do my son good to have something other than work to think about for a few hours."

For a fleeting second, Rachel wondered if Mrs. Ballinger's sly smile meant she was making plans to keep them here. But Rachel couldn't just sit on a tropical beach while there was still the possibility that bad people would go after her brother.

"I don't think Aiden and I have time for fun—"

"You have time. My husband is using his connections to sort out this virus you brought here." She nodded toward the bathroom. "I'll tell Aiden to meet you by the pool."

Rachel had never made an impromptu appearance at the parental home of a man she'd just met. The rules of engagement for this type of situation were unclear, but her gut told her that upsetting Aiden's mother would be a misstep. Better to ask Aiden what his father could do to offer to secure her family's safety. Nothing, she suspected.

Rachel thanked Aiden's mother then obediently gathered up the clothes and excused herself. She would find her own way to convince Aiden they had to leave.

Like the dress Mrs. Ballinger had insisted Rachel wear to dinner, the swimsuit hugged as if it had been made for her body. The designer shorts were a perfect fit and probably cost more than her monthly student loan payment. Rachel slid the T-shirt, silky as the sheets, over her sun-deprived skin then tucked a small section of the shirt's hem into the front of the shorts. Uneasiness churned the delicious shrimp scampi in her belly. She hadn't spent any time near the water for pleasure since the last vacation her family had taken together.

Her father had surprised the family by flying them to Brazil. Rachel remembered him telling her and Josiah about the long-nosed dolphins and how the immense volume of fresh water pouring into the ocean diluted the saltiness more than a hundred miles from shore. He'd used the line between the swirl of muddy river water pushing against the tide of blue ocean as an object lesson.

"Like people," her father said, pulling her and Josiah close, "these two very different bodies of water struggle against each other, unwilling to mix. Imagine the power if they would come together as one body." Her childish mind had thought he was merely talking about the water he'd taught her to love, but as an adult who'd had ample time to reflect on her father's words and life, she knew he had died trying to blur the lines people often drew.

Until now she hadn't realized she missed the water nearly as much as she missed her father. Cara was right. She needed to get out more. Once the virus was secured and her family was safe, she'd take a vacation. Maybe even visit Josiah and Camilla and Emma in California. Spend time on their beach. Either way, she was pretty sure stealing a deadly virus, dodging bullets, and jetting off to the Bermuda Triangle with a man she'd just met wouldn't reconnect her to the memories of the father she felt slipping further and further away.

Rachel picked up the pair of eco-friendly Chipkos sandals Aiden's mother had told her had been hand-painted by a Los Angeles artist named David Palmer.

When Rachel hadn't recognized the name, Aiden's mom had gone on to enlighten her. "Grant thought spending eighteen thousand dollars for a pair of sandals was a little ridiculous, but he calmed down when I told him the money was going to help endangered rainforest land." She'd looked Rachel in the eye. "You probably don't understand the importance of trying to save the rainforest, but it's an invaluable source of medicinal plants." She patted Rachel's slack jaw. "The sandals are supposed to be incredibly comfortable. Enjoy."

Rachel left the sandals on the bed. She'd rather go barefoot than support philanthropic claims of saving a natural resource if the end goal was the possible exploitation of those resources. Growing up in the jungle, she and her brother never wore shoes. While the bottoms of her feet had eventually turned tough as shoe leather, she never lost her tenderness toward the people who lived beneath the leafy canopy. Her father had given his life to try and help them.

Movement drew Rachel's attention to the bank of sliding glass doors. Aiden stood beside the negative-edge pool. During the day, the pool gave the illusion of dropping off into the ocean. But the underwater lights gave the chlorinated water a glow that separated it from the salty ocean the way the Amazon River separated itself from the Atlantic. He smiled and waved her out.

Rachel slid open one of the doors and stepped on the flagstone veranda, a stunning three-thousand-square-foot showpiece with clusters of plush wicker seating, an outdoor kitchen, and a twenty-foot-long dining table that overlooked a vast expanse of the water. Moonlight danced on the gentle waves that rolled against the stretch of sand at the bottom of a long staircase.

"You look like you were born for island life." Aiden had caved to his mother's pressure and changed into shorts and deck shoes, but he'd not given up his trademark white T-shirt.

"You look a lot more comfortable than you did at dinner." She could tell from the change in his expression that his discomfort had not come from his mother's supervision of his wardrobe.

"Sorry about Mom's crack about never having grandchildren." He shook his head in an embarrassed expression of apology. "She didn't mean you weren't a decent girl when she said I'm too busy chasing viruses to find a decent girl. She's just—"

"Anxious."

"Overprotective."

"You have two parents who obviously adore you." Rachel offered him a letting-you-off-the-hook smile. "You're blessed."

"I take it your mother isn't bugging you to get married, settle down, and take over the family business."

"My mother remarried, and. . .well, we don't communicate much anymore."

"Sorry to hear that." They stood side by side staring at the water, emotions rolling over her like the waves spilling onto the shore. "My mom's right about one thing. I'd be a fool to waste this chance to change your opinion of me after the *unusual* start to our relationship."

Had they started a relationship? "It's not every day I get to know someone by helping them steal a virus and catch a plane out of the country."

He shrugged and stuck his hands in his pockets. "Hey, you got a free trip to Bermuda."

"If you owned an entire chain of private islands, it wouldn't change my opinion of you."

"Is that a good thing or bad?"

"Here's what I know about you. One, you risked your life to get to the bottom of that Tibetan viral outbreak. Most people would have let those poor people die. It probably wouldn't even have made the news. Two, you left all of this"—she waved her hand toward the large stucco house with the huge wraparound porch—"and chose to live among the suffering. To make a difference in the world." She swallowed. "You remind me of my dad. . .selfless, passionate, not easily dissuaded from your calling."

"Was your dad hardheaded too?"

"Mom thought so." Rachel let her mind drift with the tide. "When our family first arrived in the Amazon, my mother loved their work among the local people. But that all changed the night my father was returning from tending a machete accident deep in the rainforest. He ran across some men working on some sort of illegal drug shipment. They beat him up and threatened to kill him if he didn't mind his own business. It scared my mother so badly, she begged my father to leave his medical clinic and take us all back to the States. She wanted him to set up a family practice in a nice safe neighborhood."

"But he wouldn't?"

It had been years, but her losses still lumped in her throat whenever she had to talk about them, including her dream of one day serving third-world people herself. "He said if he could stop even one person dying of an overdose, then maybe that's why the Lord had sent him to the jungle."

"Not sure I believe the Lord uses general practitioners to take down drug cartels."

"I believe it's possible God can use a stubborn epidemiologist to stop a worldwide pandemic."

He studied her closely, but she could tell he was really wondering if what she'd just said was true. "If that's the case, then it's a good thing I've stepped up my game."

How was it possible that someone who made up their own rules and wasn't afraid of breaking those made by others could draw her in so quickly? And yet, he had. "How does a rich kid like you end up fighting for the marginalized of this world?"

Aiden's hand went to the leather cord with three beads on his left wrist. "Long story."

"Tell me."

"Come on." He held out his hand. "I want to show you my favorite place in the world, the place where I decided years ago that I want no part of my father's plan for the Ballingers to gain world dominance."

He held her hand down the long staircase leading to a six-foot wide pier that spanned a stretch of sand made pink from thousands of years of tiny red sea creatures crushed by the powerful waves of the mid-Atlantic. Around the little cove, huge limestone rocks jutted from the water like sentinels of a private fortress. Together, she and Aiden followed the decking toward the sea until it stopped at a fan-shaped platform above the water.

He took her to the railing. "What do you think?"

"I can see why Mark Twain came here in the late 1860s and never wanted to leave."

"You know about Twain's visit?"

"I know he loved being free of harassments. The quiet of this place gave him a deep peace that allowed his conscience a rest from his 'devils' as he called them." She dragged her gaze from the water. "What devils are you running from?"

"This is what I want you to see," he said, ignoring her probing question.

At the center of the platform was a glass floor. Aiden flipped a switch on the deck railing. Underwater lights came on, providing a bird's-eye view of the nighttime activities of the colorful marine life swimming among the coral.

No wonder the man had such a fascination with science. As an only child, he'd entertained himself in his own personal nature lab. "It's stunning."

"The reef is a very delicate eco-system." Aiden dropped to his belly and invited her to do the same.

She dropped down beside him, their elbows touching, her eyes fixed on the incredible scene below.

"See how the parrot fish and angelfish exist together?" He pointed at the beautiful creatures gliding effortlessly and without note of each other. "But every so often, a Portuguese man-of-war will try to infiltrate their serenity." He pointed to a jelly-like blob moving in on the happy world. "They're a harmless looking glob, but in truth—"

"Their tentacles can deal a deadly sting."

"Exactly." He rolled over on his back, pillowed his head on his interlaced fingers, and looked at the stars twinkling in the velvety sky. "I fell in love with the idea that nature holds the key to so many things. I thought if I could unlock the secrets, I could keep the world's men-of-war from destroying the beauty."

Rachel rolled onto her side and faced him. "Like giant viruses."

"Like the killer virus I found in Tibet." Moonlight lit more than his features. It lit the depths of his soul.

She could imagine a lonely boy lying out here for hours, longing to connect to something greater than himself. This was a contemplation she understood. After her mother moved her and Josiah back to Kansas, she'd married a wheat farmer. Lonely, bored, and far removed from the land she'd grown up in, Rachel had spent many a starry night lying in the middle of her stepfather's wheat field and wishing for the exact same thing. "What are you going to do?"

"I'm going to disappoint my father." The pain in Aiden's voice let her know he'd not come to this decision easily.

"How?"

Aiden rolled to face her, propping his head on his bent elbow. "My dad owns Gaumond Technology, including Gaumond Labs, and a number of other companies."

Rachel bolted upright. "What?"

"You work for my father."

"I don't—"

Aiden sat up so now they were eye to eye. "We *both* work for my father."

"But you're a virus hunter. With a team."

"Dad humored my virus hunting sort of the way some parents allow their children to backpack around Europe—you know, a phase they hope their kid will outgrow. Anyway, I talked him into funding the Rapid Response Support Team."

"Your father pays for your research trips?"

"Yes."

"And for things like your suite at the Watergate? Private charters? Lear jets?"

"All of it."

"Why?"

"He's trying to buy my loyalty." Aiden's eyes implored her to understand. "He wants me to come in from the field and take over some portion of the company. He says if I wear a suit for a few years I'll make enough money to buy a private island of my own."

"Do you want your own island?"

"I don't want any part of his plan. As soon as I figure out how to render this virus useless, I'm going to work for Doctors Without Borders. I've already sent in my paperwork and been hired."

Rachel felt the dreams she'd buried deep within herself sprout. A vine of hope leapt from her heart and drew her toward Aiden as if he were a source of light she must have. Desire pushed away her well-trained self-control. Without taking the time to gather all the facts or weigh all the consequences, she leaned in and kissed him. He smelled of soap and tasted of salty sea spray and hope. Between the two of them, perhaps her father's dream of changing the world could be realized.

Aiden hesitated, then took her into his arms and kissed her back.

When she finally broke the kiss, he gulped and sat back. "Whoa. I didn't know geeky girls could kiss like that."

"Geeky girls have many talents, but. . ." Her smile faded. "I shouldn't have done that. I'm sorry."

"I didn't mind."

She stood up and started walking. "I do. This isn't some romantic winter holiday. There are lives hanging in the balance here."

"I know. And my dad was right about one thing."

"The virus needs to be cloned."

"Exactly. But I can't let him send this sample back to our lab after what's happened."

"What are you thinking?"

"I need to take the sample to an old mentor of mine."

"Who?"

"Charlie Zimmern."

"You're taking a rare and potentially fatal virus to the crazy Frenchman who lost his medical license in a very public scandal?"

"That was a setup. I'm sure of it. Charlie's the only one I trust with this."

"He disappeared after that cloning debacle, and if he's as smart as he claims to be, he'll never let himself be found."

"He's in Istanbul."

She wanted to ask how he knew, how he could be sure, but she could tell from his face that he'd never lost contact with his mentor. "When are you leaving?"

"Tonight. I've already stowed the virus on the plane. I just need to tell my father."

"I'm going with you."

"No. You'll be safer here. No one will think to look for you out of the country, and if they do, you'll be surrounded by a crackerjack security team."

"You're not leaving me with your mother."

"I'm not taking you to Turkey. No telling what I'll find there."

"Wait." Rachel put her hand on his arm. "Do you hear that?"

"Jet Skis." Aiden ran to the edge of the deck. "Coming from the mainland." He wheeled and grabbed her hand. "We've got to get back to the house. Warn my parents."

Rachel tripped as they ran along the boardwalk, pulling Aiden down with her. Bullets sang over their heads. When there was a break in the firing, they ran.

ELEVEN

Aiden's fingers tightened around Rachel's as they ran back down the pier then through a row of palm trees and away from the exposed shoreline. Adrenaline pumped through him fast as the round of bullets he'd just heard. How had they found them here? And how was he going to warn his parents?

Darkness had settled over the island, leaving the beaming moon as their only source of light as he led her up the sandy dune to Cook's Peak. From that vantage point, they should be able to see the house and what was going on before deciding what their next move would be.

At the top of the peak, he crouched down next to her, but this time it wasn't to enjoy the scenery. This time they were fighting for their lives. He searched the shadows in the clearing below for movement, making the logical assumption that the intruders had gone straight to the house.

"I can't believe you planned to leave me," Rachel whispered.

He forced the guilt down. "I thought you'd be safe here."

"Obviously, I'm not. Is there a way to contact your parents?"

"Not from here, but the guards will have heard the gunshots. We have contingency plans for a situation like this, including two hidden safe rooms in the house, but for the moment, we're the vulnerable ones out here in the open."

Two figures, dressed in black and carrying weapons, emerged from the cover of the foliage and headed for the house. He caught sight of two more figures moving through the trees along the side of the house.

"How many do you see?" he whispered.

"Four," she said.

"Me too."

Their options at this point were severely limited. There was no way they could make it back down the rise and to the open area around the house without being seen. To the right was the boat launch, but the lack of cover ruled out going that direction.

The clouds momentarily blocked the moon, then slipped past again. Someone shouted. Two of the intruders were moving toward the house while the second pair turned and headed in the direction of the airfield, which lay behind them. The men were spreading out. Searching. . .

"We need to get to the plane." He pulled Rachel to her feet.

"What about your parents?"

"I can radio the house from the plane."

He knew the risks of leaving his parents. If the intruders discovered the virus wasn't in the house, things could easily morph into a hostage situation. Hopefully his parents' security team would react before it came to that. Moonlight guided them back down the sandy ridge toward the airstrip, and they were careful to stay in the shadows. The plane appeared untouched when they arrived, but he knew once he fired the engines, the intruders would figure out where they'd gone. If nothing else, the diversion would give his parents time to get out.

He helped Rachel into the cockpit then climbed into the pilot's seat. Headset on, he powered up the radio so he could contact his parents, simultaneously running through the mental start-up checklist. He was going to need to be ready to fly out of here the moment his parents made it to the plane.

He fumbled with the radio until he finally heard his father's voice crackling through the speaker. "Aiden. . .where are you?"

"They blocked our way back to the house. Made it to the plane."

"And Rachel?"

"She's with me." He hesitated. "The virus is on the plane too."

"It's not in the house?"

"No."

"Aiden. . ."

He saw movement out of the corner of his eye. Armed men in black wet suits were coming toward the plane.

Aiden started the engine. "They found us."

"You need to get off the island," his father said.

"I'm not leaving you behind—"

"We won't make it in time," his father said. "We're in one of the safe rooms, and the guards are with us. We'll be fine. You need to leave. Contact me when you land. I have faith in you."

"Dad! I'm not leaving without—"

"He's right, Aiden. You need to get out." He could hear his mother in the background. "Saving the virus isn't worth losing your life. It's not worth any of our lives."

Radio contact dropped.

They were on their own.

Shots sounded outside the jet.

"Aiden, they're coming."

"Okay." Flaps up, he turned on the lights then started taxiing down the runway.

Guilt dug at him for dragging his parents into this and now leaving them behind. He never should have brought his troubles to their door. Maybe his father was right. He should have stood up to his responsibilities to the family company and let someone else do the groundwork. But now wasn't the time to drum up old regrets. Bullets showered the tarmac around them.

"Fasten your seat belt," he told Rachel. "We're getting out of here."

He caught the fear on her face as the plane hurtled down the runway. This hadn't been a part of his plan. He thought she'd be safe here. Clearly, he'd been wrong. A minute later, they were airborne and leaving the small island behind.

To Aiden's relief, Rachel waited for the plane to level off before saying anything. "How did they find us?"

"I don't know," he said, mentally retracing his steps, wondering which move had given him away. "I guess it wouldn't be that hard to trace me to my father. Maybe they assumed I would come here for help."

"Then it has to be someone who knows you. Or someone your father talked to today. Though I didn't know your family owned a private island, and I've read everything there is to read about you." She adjusted her headset. "Who knows about your parents' vacation home in Bermuda?"

He shrugged. "Most of my dad's business associates."

"We'll make a list." She set her jaw toward the place on the horizon where the stars met the sea. "Then once we're home. . ." She turned to face him. "You are taking me home, right?"

He cut her a sly glance. "Have to make a little detour first."

"You're still not thinking about going to see Charlie, are you?"

He hesitated with his answer. "As far as I'm concerned, he's our only option right now."

"You really trust him?"

"I've known Charlie since I was a kid. He's the one who inspired me to be a virus hunter. He might be a bit eccentric, but yes. I'd trust him with my life."

Which meant she was going to have to trust him.

"I got the impression your father wouldn't agree with that decision after the comments between the two of you at dinner."

"Charlie and my father haven't spoken in years, but Charlie can help us, and he's off the grid."

"How far off the grid?"

"Far enough that whoever wants this virus won't be able to find us."

"You know the kind of equipment we're going to need."

"Charlie's been working on a number of *unofficial* projects and has the resources."

He could see her putting two and two together, but instead of asking who Charlie worked for and who financed him, she said, "I still think this is crazy." Her hand brushed his arm. "We need to go straight to the authorities and let them deal with this."

"Then what happens with the virus? Or your brother and his family?" He hated using the implied threat, but he'd come to realize he needed all the help he could get. "We don't have time to jump through a bunch of hoops."

"My brother has a little girl. Emma—"

"Charlie is our best bet," he said.

"If anything happens to her or—"

"What I know is that I haven't been able to contact my team, and I can't do on my own what needs to be done to put a cork in this bottle I've opened. With yours and Charlie's help, we can do more than save your brother's family. We can save the world."

He wasn't sure who he was trying to convince, Rachel or himself. But he scanned the illuminated dials, thankful he was comfortable flying at night. In fact, he preferred a traffic-free sky and a star-lit trek, but soon enough he would be flying into the glare of the sun and the possibility this was a problem even Charlie couldn't cipher.

"Okay," Rachel said, breaking into his thoughts. "I'll help, but first I need to apologize."

"You don't need to apologize for anything."

She held up her palm. "I'm not sure what I was thinking when I kissed you. It was a mistake. We clearly live in two very different worlds. I live in a three-room rental, have student loans to pay, and am saving to buy a house one day. Your family owns a jet, an island, and a major research corporation. Do you know how much the sandals cost that your mom wanted me to wear?"

He glanced at her. "More than your car."

"Yes." She grinned. "This is a world I could never live in. It's not a world I want to live in."

So that was how she saw him. A spoiled kid playing games with people's lives. It was why he'd never brought a girl to meet his parents. Maybe trying to live in both worlds wasn't possible.

"I might have been born into money, but that doesn't define who I am."

"I didn't say it did. I'm sorry if that came across judgmental. It's just that I'm scared, and overwhelmed, and I really don't know how to deal with all of this."

"Honestly, I don't either." He stared into the clouds building ahead, but his mind was drifting back to the few sunny, carefree days he remembered of his childhood. "Whenever I think of safe, I think of the island. Every year, we went there for a few weeks to escape the East Coast winters. From the moment our plane touched down, I had my parents' full attention. Dad didn't have work, and Mom didn't have her committee meetings. All we had was each other."

"I'm sorry, I—"

"Kissing you was like escaping the snow and loneliness all over again."

"Please don't go there," she whispered, her eyes wet in the lights of the dashboard.

"Okay." He picked up his radio. "At some point, we're going to have to trust someone. But listen. . ." The lights of the big island of Bermuda sparkled against the horizon. "You don't have to come with me. When we set down, I can put you on a flight to wherever you want to go. Just say the word. You could go to your brother's or your mother."

"If I'm right about what the torn photo meant, I don't want them linked to me at all."

"Moreno told me how good you are at your job. You'll be an asset to the great amount of work Charlie and I have to do."

"I hope we're not about to make a big mistake."

He stared out at the night sky, working through the details in his mind as they flew across the water. With or without her, he knew this was what he was going to have to do. When they landed, he'd ditch this jet and charter another private flight to Istanbul. He'd need to get the required visas in order to get into Turkey, but it was all doable. They could be there in twelve hours, still giving them a small margin of time to work with their samples.

Maybe she was right and his solution was a big mistake, but as far as he was concerned, there was only one option. Charlie Zimmern.

TWELVE

Three flights up, Aiden stopped in front of apartment 404. The click of a lock releasing silenced Rachel's mental argument with herself. Whatever waited behind this door, she would not be a part of it if it crossed her ethical lines. The grate of a metal chain sliding through rings was followed by the releasing of several bolts. Finally, the knob turned and the door opened just a crack.

Huge gray eyes blinked behind the magnified lenses and heavy black frames perched upon the twitching nose of an old man assessing whether or not to take the bait. "Who is she?"

"Dr. Rachel Allen." Rachel stepped forward. "Epidemiologist and viral researcher." If he tried to pull something shady, she wanted him to know he wasn't dealing with an untrained fool.

"We'll see if you're as smart as Aiden has always claimed you are." Charlie opened the door wide enough for Rachel to get her first glimpse of the man whose formulas and theories she'd studied in school.

Charlie Zimmern, a man whose scientific contributions had made him as big as the universe in her mind, was in real life a short little fellow with a thick cloud of snowy white hair, meticulously parted and combed. He wore a heavy gray sweater with all five large black buttons neatly buttoned. But as her gaze took in the rest of him, the man she'd idolized seemed to deteriorate as if nothing but his brilliant mind and beating heart mattered. Wrinkled chinos hung from his twig-like bowed legs, and his wing-tipped shoes were scuffed and threaded with kite string instead of proper laces. The idea that the world's greatest biochemist and geneticist was a mere mortal was a magnet that drew Rachel a step forward.

"Come." He waved them in then stuck his head over the threshold and looked both ways. Satisfied they'd not been followed, he closed them in then bolted all the locks and refastened the chain.

The three of them stood just inside the locked door as she and Dr. Zimmern sized each other up. The smell of rancid olive oil, strong coffee, and takeout boxes that should have been trashed days ago pressed into Rachel's evaluation. She clutched the handle of her carry-on. Aiden clutched the strap of the insulated cooler that held the virus, and Dr. Zimmern clutched the very real possibility they'd brought trouble to his door.

Rachel eased her gaze from Dr. Zimmern's magnified scrutiny and slowly took in the room with the curtains drawn tight over the windows. Neat stacks of books and papers covered the floor, surrounding a small couch and rocking chair and two metal chairs at the sagging kitchen table. On the coffee table, she noticed an unfinished jigsaw puzzle of a map of ocean topography. A finished puzzle of a map of the Sahara filled the kitchen tabletop. On the small kitchen counter was a completed puzzle map of some sort of mountain range, perhaps the Alps. Aiden had warned her of Charlie Zimmern's eccentricities. He'd been right.

Rachel's gaze skipped over the organized clutter and traveled up the walls. Complicated formulas written in chalk, pencil, and black marker covered every available inch of the chipped plaster. She recognized $E=mc^2$, energy equals mass times the speed of light squared, but the rest were scribblings well beyond anything she could decipher. . .and she was good at math and chemistry.

"How have you been, Charlie?" Aiden asked.

"Busy." He smiled. "My viruses keep me busy."

"Viruses? Here?" The word croaked from Rachel's suddenly very dry throat.

Charlie motioned for Aiden to hand over the insulated cooler draped over his shoulder. "Let me see the virus you wish to clone."

"How did you know we wanted a virus cloned?" Rachel asked as Aiden deposited the insulated cooler on the table.

"You are here, aren't you? Tell me what we have and what you need."

Aiden filled him in on the frozen woolly mammoth with the strange anomalies in his heart, the subsequent death of the Tibetans who'd uncovered the extinct creature, and his suspicions that the two of these things were connected. "I need the virus stabilized so that we can develop a vaccine or an effective cure."

Aiden told the old man about the loss of the original source of the virus and what Rachel had learned about the virus's ability to replicate at a rapid speed in vertebrates. He left out the part about them stealing the last remaining sample from Gaumond Labs and being shot at twice.

"Cloning will give you that ability. But the process is highly regulated. Why come here? What aren't you telling me?"

"There are people after this virus. People we believe plan to use it to develop a super virus."

"The technology is already here. They don't have to have the actual virus. All they need is the virus's genomic blueprint."

"So what do we do?" Rachel asked. "All it would take is an accidental leak or misuse during the research getting into the wrong hands, and this could spread."

Charlie lifted his chin until his glasses returned to their proper place on his nose. "What is the viability of the virus?"

"Thirty-two hours at best," Aiden said.

"And how many samples are left?"

Aiden hesitated. "This is it."

"I'm assuming you're funding this on your own, correct?" Charlie asked, grinning at Aiden.

"I'll take care of you, old man." The smile they exchanged confirmed Rachel's earlier suspicions that Charlie Zimmern was more than a mentor to Aiden.

Charlie seemed lost in thought, about what Rachel could only guess.

Aiden nudged him. "We're kind of in a hurry, Charlie."

"*Noisette* first and something to eat."

"*Noisette*?" Rachel asked.

"I work better with a fresh cup of espresso."

Charlie headed toward the kitchen.

"Aiden?" Rachel whispered. "He's a loose cannon."

"Charlie marches to his own beat, but he can do this in his sleep." He held out his hand. "I trust him."

Rachel had no choice but to leave her suitcase and follow Charlie and Aiden to the small kitchen, but her nerves were too tightly wound to allow her to stand still while Charlie heated water on a hot plate. She wandered the maze of books and journals to work off her anxiety. Several of the scientific magazines had a younger Charlie Zimmern on the cover, and most of the textbooks had his name on the spine. Aiden was right. If anyone could accomplish what they were asking, it was Dr. Zimmern. She needed to relax. Trust the man God had led them to.

Once they'd finished a cup of Turkish coffee turned hazelnut color by all the milk Charlie had added and several thick slices of pistachio baklava, he motioned them to a door on the far side of the room.

"Come," he said. "And bring your project."

Charlie stopped outside the closed door, reached inside his sweater, and pulled out a key dangling from a string around his neck. He unlocked the door then stepped inside. Rachel was expecting a small bedroom, but instead she stepped into a huge, brilliantly lit, fully equipped state-of-the-art laboratory. Every piece of equipment on the well-organized eight-foot worktable was clean and precisely placed. Beneath the glass hood of the biosafety cabinet, several racks were filled with glittering vials, all in different stages of replication.

"My work," Charlie announced proudly as he shuffled to the biosafety cabinet and pointed to the vials.

Questions swirled in Rachel's head. How did a man stripped of his research credentials end up with a fully-equipped lab? "What is this place?"

"My office," Charlie said.

Across the room, Charlie's framed medical school diploma hung askew on the pristine white wall. Rachel reached to straighten it and in doing so reminded her that the oath they'd all sworn when they had received their medical degrees meant they were to do good rather than harm. Charlie Zimmern should not be practicing any type of research.

"Leave it," Charlie said as if he'd read her mind.

"But it's crooked," was all she could think to say. The only thing in the lab askew she wanted to add, but didn't.

"It meant a lot to my mother when I became a doctor." If Charlie was bitter, as she would have been after having so many years of study and unfulfilled dreams flushed down the toilet, it did not sound in his voice. Instead, he repeated the fact as if it were merely part of a solvable equation.

All of this, his life's work, this lab in a forgotten corner of the world, his willingness to help them, all of it had been to please his mother? Realization that she'd devoted her own life to medical research in the hopes that somehow it would have made her father proud hit her hard in the gut.

Once they were all properly suited up, Charlie removed the tape sealing the cooler then asked Rachel to set a water bath to thaw the samples. To Rachel's surprise, when she rattled off the number he was looking for from her earlier examination of the concentration of the virus in the fluid, Charlie smiled and said, "You'll do nicely."

She fought back the urge to say she wasn't a first-year researcher, but allowing her preconceptions of a man to tank a possible solution, maybe even the only solution, to this big problem wasn't the answer. She decided to put her aversions and suspicions aside and see what she could learn.

Charlie moved about the lab like a man half his age, as if being elbow deep in science was his personal fountain of youth. Between each dilution, she helped him change pipet tips.

He passed a vial to Rachel. "Rock gently to mix. Do not swirl."

"Then incubate at 37°C for one to two hours," Rachel said.

Charlie cut her a pleased glance. "I've experimented with different incubation periods. According to the data I've amassed, one hour exactly is the magic number."

His precision in the lab gave her a remarkable sense of peace. His kindness as he directed her reminded her of how her father used to walk her through experiments of building volcanoes whose eruptions were fueled by baking soda.

Rachel set the timer then eagerly got to work helping Charlie microwave agarose to a boil and place the tubes in a water bath to prevent solidification of the base. When the timer dinged, Charlie checked the agarose. Satisfied that the base was not hot enough to kill the virus, he carefully overlaid the cells.

"Now we wait another hour." He started the timer himself then perched upon a stool.

Needing something to fill the time, Rachel decided to tidy up the workspace. She discarded formaldehyde and unused agarose plugs into an appropriate chemical waste container. Then she added crystal violet staining solution to each plate, enough to cover the wells.

"What do you think we're looking at, Charlie?" Aiden asked.

"Not a known adenovirus." Charlie's voice was muffled by the helmet he still wore. "Of the more than one hundred viruses in the Adenovirus genus, approximately forty-nine are known to cause human disease, heart muscle infection, and heart muscle dysfunction." Charlie drummed his fingers on the counter, as if lost in thought. "You're right. They'll come for this one."

Rachel dropped the empty beaker she held, glass shattering on the tiled floor. "Who will come?"

Charlie turned his helmet toward her. "The same people who came for me."

THIRTEEN

They'll come for this one.

Charlie's words haunted Aiden over the next two days. While he continued to check the results of the yeast cell system which facilitated a rapid response to the fast-spreading virus, Charlie and Rachel poured over the data they'd accumulated. It was a game of hurry up and wait as the blossoming colonies started to appear on the plates.

The process of cloning a virus wasn't new to any of them. The more labs working on diagnostic testing theoretically meant a quicker timeline of stopping the effects of a virus through drugs and vaccines. And the ability to stabilize the virus outside the body meant the possibility of developing those new treatments. The problem faced in creating a synthetic virus was that the very same technology behind stopping a pandemic could be used to create a bioweapon. In the wrong hands, a virus that had resurrected itself after lying dormant for centuries could be catastrophic. Which brought up another problem they were facing. Working on the virus in Charlie's lab was only part of the solution. Until they identified whoever was behind the attempts to steal the virus, the world would remain at risk.

Aiden glanced at the clock on the wall when they finally stepped out of the lab and into the darkened apartment, surprised it was already past eight.

Charlie flipped on a few lights then pulled out his phone. "I'll order some delivery. We've been cooped up in that lab long enough and besides, there's nothing more we can do tonight but wait."

Rachel tugged on the bottom of her T-shirt. "I think I'll shower before dinner if no one minds."

"Don't forget, you have three minutes." Charlie nodded toward the hallway as he placed the call. "Then hot water is gone."

"Three minutes," Rachel repeated. "Got it."

Aiden smiled at Rachel's easy acceptance of Charlie's idiosyncrasies as he walked to the large window. The way they'd seamlessly fallen into working with each other had certainly made the time they'd spent in the lab valuable, but so many unanswered questions as to who was planning what with this virus remained. He rolled his shoulders slowly, trying to unravel some of the kinks the stress had formed.

He peered through the drawn curtains. Lights of a dozen apartment buildings and streetlights shone in the distance as night settled in around them. Coming to Charlie had been the right call. He was sure of it now. Not only was the virus safe, but they were making progress ensuring they had a viable clone. But time was running out. At some point they were going to have to trust someone outside their little circle.

He waited for Charlie to finish making their dinner order and get off the phone before he turned back to him. "I'm still paying Evan to find out who set you up."

"Forget it." Charlie waved off the suggestion. "You've already done enough for me, Aiden."

"Clearly I haven't." He shook his head. "Going into hiding was supposed to be temporary."

"As long as I can continue my research, does it matter that I no longer have the title that goes with that diploma on the wall?"

"But eventually it's going to catch up to you. We don't exactly have permission to do what we're doing. Do you know how many regulations we've broken?" Aiden worked to keep the frustration out of his voice, but he was tired of feeling so out of control. "You need to be back in the States, leading our team."

"At least we know we're the good guys."

Aiden frowned. He wasn't sure that was going to be enough. "When this all comes out eventually, that's not going to matter."

"Thanks to you, this isn't exactly a backstreet lab. We're prepared to handle the work. Besides, what choice did you really have?"

Compromising biosafety had never been a risk either of them had been willing to take when they'd set up the workspace, but that didn't relieve any of his uneasiness over what they were doing.

"Did you hear from your father?" Charlie asked, changing the subject.

"I messaged him on your encrypted line. He and Mom made it safely to Bermuda then returned to our island with the police. The damage done to the property was minimal, but the last I heard they still have no idea who was behind the attack. Dad's working with the police to get answers."

Charlie grabbed his coat, then hesitated. "Does he know you're working with me?"

"He's knows we're safe, but I don't want to take any chances. I figure the less he knows the better, for his own protection."

Charlie took off his glasses and rubbed the bridge of his nose. "You know we can clone the virus, but after that. . .We're going to have to get a bigger team involved if we're actually going to stop the virus. But in the meantime, I've an errand to run."

"What about dinner? Aren't you hungry?"

"I'm not exactly used to eating on a schedule. Though you won't be alone." Charlie nodded toward the bathroom. "I like her. If I were thirty years younger, I'd definitely have my eye on her."

"My job doesn't really have room for a relationship right now."

"Haven't you thought about settling down? Maybe try a more traditional job?"

"You sound like my father."

"Maybe he's right."

"You never settled down, Charlie."

"I'm far too set in my ways for most women."

Aiden glanced around the cluttered apartment with its stacks of research papers and books. "I've seen behind that crusty shell of yours.

You're nothing but a teddy bear on the inside. I'm not ready for the office and a suit and tie."

"You're never going to be ready," Charlie said. "You were born for fieldwork."

"I learned from the best."

Charlie's gaze drifted toward the sounds of Rachel finishing her shower. "I've watched the two of you work together over the past couple of days. She's good for you."

"Maybe." He glanced down the hall where she'd disappeared, wishing he could forget their kiss. "We're too different."

"Why do you say that?"

"She told me. I think she's having a hard time seeing past the spoiled rich kid in me." Aiden reached for a handful of pistachios from a bowl on the coffee table and popped one into his mouth. "I can't really blame her. No matter how hard I try, I can't shed that part of me."

"Your past will always be a part of you. Maybe it's time you accepted yourself for who you are. Who's to say you can't embrace both sides?"

By the time the food came, Rachel had pulled on a pair of gray sweatpants and a zippered hoodie. She joined Aiden in the living room that now smelled like spicy lamb meat.

"Feel better?" Aiden asked, trying not to stare at how naturally beautiful she looked with wet hair and no makeup.

"Definitely. Where's Charlie?"

"He had to run an errand."

She looked out at the darkened skyline and the lights of the city. "What kind of errand?"

"I trust him, Rachel. We have to trust him."

"I know. I'm just having a hard time not seeing a villain around every corner." She studied the food he'd spread out on the small table. "This looks amazing."

"The paper plates and card table, or the food?" he teased.

She managed a laugh. "Definitely the food. What is it?"

"*Pide* is the Turkish version of pizza," he said, opening up the box.

"Flat bread with meat, vegetables, and cheese toppings. Sometimes eggs, a sprinkle of lemon. . ."

"And this?"

"*Döner.* Marinated lamb that's been cooked on a spit, then sliced and eaten in a pita with tomato, pepper, and onion."

She slid into one of the chairs before grabbing a slice of the *pide* and taking a bite. "Wow. This is good." They ate until Rachel broke their comfortable silence. "I have a question for you."

"Shoot."

"I'm having a hard time seeing your parents eating delivery on paper plates. I mean, they bought an island as a second home. And yet you travel to places like Tibet, live in a tent, and seem just as comfortable eating Turkish pizza in a tiny apartment as you do flying a jet halfway around the world and dining on sautéed shrimp in some tropical paradise." She cocked her head. "I'm just. . .trying to figure you out."

He took a bite of marinated lamb then wiped his fingers. "In other words, you want to know how a spoiled rich kid decided he wanted to do humanitarian work."

"That's not exactly what I said."

He tried to read her expression. Kissing him had clearly been an impulsive act she regretted. Now he wasn't sure what she thought of him. "But it's what you were thinking?"

"Maybe."

"My father had these grand plans for me to run the company, and although I enjoyed my science classes much more than my business classes all through college, it was simply what was expected. I honestly never really thought about anything else."

"So what changed?"

"Charlie, actually. As you can imagine, he never liked working in the office. He was always traveling the world, following pandemics, and involved in cutting-edge technology. One summer he asked me to go with him."

"You'd traveled before."

"Yes. In five-star hotels with room service. Traveling with Charlie was different." He squeezed a slice of lemon on his slice of *pide*, then took a bite "We were in Zambia at the time, working on an outbreak of cholera. I'd spent hours in a makeshift lab as we tested to find the source of the contamination that was decimating the surrounding villages."

"I'm guessing the place was short on five-star hotels."

"Ha. No, that wasn't it. Charlie came to me after dinner one night and told me a woman had just showed up at the hospital. She'd walked two hours just to get to the hospital to ask for help for her sick son. Charlie wanted me to come with him to check on the outbreak in their village. We drove through the bush in the dark with a guide who somehow managed to hit every pothole on that narrow dirt road. I'll admit, I'd never been so uncomfortable in my entire life. But then I met Samuel. He told me he was thirteen, but he didn't look like he was a day over nine."

"Did he live?" she asked.

Aiden tugged the bracelet on his arm. "He did. He gave me this as a thank-you. I've never forgotten him. Not too long after that, I talked to my dad about starting an official rapid response team through his company. I came up with an entire plan, including partnering with a couple of universities."

"What did he think about that?"

"He decided to placate me. Thought it would be good publicity, but that I would get bored quickly of roughing it."

"But you didn't."

"No, and now my father expects me to give it all up."

"Does he know about your plans with Doctors Without Borders?"

"I haven't told him."

Her brow rose. "Sometimes you have to take a leap of faith and trust God to do the impossible with our lives."

He shook his head. "You don't know my father."

"No, but I met him, and I can tell he loves you and is proud of you."

"There won't be forgiveness for walking away from the company my father built from nothing."

"Maybe he just needs time to let it sink in."

"He's had plenty of time. Trust me."

Aiden's phone went off. "Excuse me, but I'm waiting to hear from my dad. I'm hoping he has some answers as to who's behind the attacks." He checked the secure message system Charlie had set up for his emails.

"Is it him?"

"No." Aiden paused at the sender's name. "It's a message from Iceman."

"What is it?"

Aiden looked up at Rachel. "Apparently, he's been trying to contact me. He says he has some answers I need. He'll be in Istanbul in the morning. Says we need to meet somewhere safe."

FOURTEEN

Rachel was dressed and reading an article Charlie had written nearly ten years ago on the advantages of cloning viruses when Aiden stepped from the tiny bathroom dressed in his usual worn jeans, white T-shirt, and hiking boots. His hair was wet, but he hadn't taken the time to shave.

"Morning," he said, totally oblivious to how his low-maintenance style appealed to a girl who always chose comfort over impressing others.

His allure had already gone up several notches on her interest meter after several days of watching him work in Charlie's lab. It wasn't every day a girl got a backstage pass into the brilliant mind of the hero in her chosen field. In fact, the time she'd spent working on the virus with Aiden and Charlie, each of them taking turns on the loveseat to catch a little sleep and eating takeout from a box, had been eye-opening on so many levels.

Not only had she learned the intricacies of a cloning technique she would have sworn was only possible in the imagination of a sci-fi novel writer, she'd come to realize she'd misjudged both Aiden and Charlie. She'd judged them in the very same way people often judged her as a goody-two-shoes missionary kid based on what her father had done.

She'd labeled Aiden a spoiled rich kid and Charlie a rogue scientist. She was wrong. On both counts.

Charlie was kind, patient with her, even when she struggled to follow his unconventional reasoning or figure the correct answers to one of his complicated equations, and he was always telling her how good she was at her work. Every time he looked over her shoulder to check her progress, he gave her shoulder an approving pat. His touch reminded her of her father, made her feel as if her dad was there, cheering her on. She was a bee drawn to the nectar of the old man's approval.

And Aiden, selfless and generous in both his funding of this entire operation and his determination to stop this virus before it spread throughout the world, had made her feel secure in the likelihood that together they would do something significant. Now and in the future. He'd said more than once that he needed her to help contain this virus and what a great addition she'd been to his team. Whether or not he thought about their kiss, she couldn't say, because he hadn't mentioned it. Not even once. But the last few days he seemed to linger when he brushed past her in the small lab or when their hands touched during the exchange of cell vials. His constant and close proximity had ignited the smoldering embers left over from their kiss into a flame that was pushing her out onto Charlie's chilly balcony more and more often.

"Rachel?" Aiden pulled on the sweater he'd picked up from a vendor's stall during one of his food runs. "You okay?"

She shook herself free of the dream that they might have a future together after this was over. "Just nervous about meeting your friend."

"Iceman has been my wingman since college. But I told you, I'll go on my own. You'd be safer—"

"No. I need to get out and stretch my legs. Besides that, you might need someone to watch your back."

He shot her a half smile. "You can't really say you've seen Istanbul if you haven't strolled the Grand Bazaar."

"That might be true, but here's what I don't understand. How did Iceman find you?"

"Iceman knows me like a brother. He also knows my high regard for Charlie. It wouldn't take much for him to put two and two together."

Trust didn't come easy for her, she had to admit, but something felt wrong about this. "If he knew you'd come to Charlie, why didn't he just come here?"

"He knows Charlie's in Istanbul. But you're the first person I've brought here." The trust he conveyed in his gaze didn't completely tamp her concerns, but Aiden was right. They were going to need help to see this through.

She gave Charlie an impromptu kiss on the cheek before they left. The old man, who smelled of strong coffee and leftover lamb, had a smile on his face as he assured them of his commitment to check on the progress of their work. Outside his door, they waited until they heard every bolt and chain lock into place.

Aiden took her hand. "Better if we look like a couple."

To keep from concentrating on the heat generated by his touch, Rachel rehashed the plan they'd agreed on. They'd spent the last few days working with the rules and predictably of science. Adding someone else to this risky pursuit was fraught with unpredictability. She'd argued against it. Even laid out all the things that could go wrong. But in the end, Aiden had smiled at her and said, "Life isn't always predictable. But I know Iceman, and we can trust him."

They planned to arrive at least thirty minutes earlier than the scheduled time for the meet. They'd wait at a table in the back of a pastry shop and order two *noisettes*. Once Iceman arrived, Aiden would make certain his friend had not been followed. If Aiden saw or suspected anything suspicious, they'd slip out the back of the shop. As a precaution, in case they got separated, he'd given her a burner phone and some cash, but if anything went wrong, they were going to have to warn Charlie to pack up the cloned virus and disappear using the escape route known only to Charlie. Once the old man was safely out of harm's way, he was to contact Aiden via the burner phone he'd purchased from a vendor beside the red cart where he had purchased their morning fix of simit rolls.

"First stop," Aiden said to her after they descended the stairs of Charlie's apartment house and stepped into the crisp air. "A transportation kiosk."

Aiden was either excited or anxious to have his team back together. Although he'd allowed her a small peek into who he really was, she wasn't sure she knew him well enough to gauge which emotion had the stronger pull. She zipped up her long jacket and rubbed the toe of one of her boots over the back of her black jeans as she waited for him to buy an *Istanbulkart*, a contactless electronic card he'd said could be used on the many modes of public transportation across the city.

They casually inserted themselves into the crowd heading toward a bus stop and hopped aboard the first metrobus that came along. The diesel vehicle coughed black smoke and was crammed with so many people they had to stand. Aiden's breath warmed the back of her neck and his arm encircled her waist to keep her upright during the sudden stops and turns through the traffic. Rachel noticed there were no route maps posted anywhere inside the bus. When she turned to mention the possibility to Aiden that they could get lost, he merely tightened his hold on her.

After several blocks, Aiden whispered in her ear that this is where they would get off to catch the public ferry. The orange and white chimneys of the passenger boat bobbed in the choppy blue waters. Aiden placed their card on the electronic reader on top of the turnstile, and she followed him to the upper deck of the ferry.

"Would you like a little history lesson?" he asked, passing rows of wooden benches before stopping at the rail that overlooked the water.

"I would," she said, welcoming the distraction.

"The city of Istanbul actually lies partly in Europe and partly in Asia."

Rachel glanced up at him. "Now how did I miss that fact growing up?"

Aiden let out a low laugh. "I don't know, because you don't miss much." The same could easily be said about him. "The city's separated by the Bosphorus Strait, which connects the Sea of Marmara and the Black Sea."

"You really have traveled the world, haven't you?"

"Thanks to my parents. They took me to Cairo, Paris, and Berlin, you name it, but I've always been partial to this city."

"Is that why you set Charlie up here?"

"That and he already knew the city well."

"I wish we were just tourists today." The wind whipped at her hair. "I've never seen anything like this."

She took a deep breath as she scanned the horizon, thankful to be outside in the fresh air. Gulls circled the boat. The heavily populated city, lush with centuries of churches, mosques, and other architecture, spread out along the waterfront. A week wouldn't be enough to explore the city properly. But all she could think about right now was staying alive.

"I first came here with my parents when I was seventeen." Aiden broke into her thoughts. "I wanted to go skiing in Aspen, but my father had friends living here, and they invited us to stay for the holidays."

"How did that turn out?"

"They had a daughter, Gabriella. They must have bribed her into showing me the city. She was in college and studying history. We visited museums, churches, mosques. Spent hours in the Grand Bazaar and Basilica Cistern. She somehow managed to unlock a love of history in me."

"So was it the city that fascinated you, or Gabriella?"

"I suppose a little of both." He laughed then turned and caught her gaze. "I'll have to bring you back here someday. There are so many things I'd love to show you."

There are so many things I'd love for you to show me.

Rachel kept her thoughts to herself. She'd meant what she said about the two of them being too different. These feelings were nothing more than admiration. And kissing him had been a foolish impulse.

Twenty minutes later they disembarked at the ferry terminal. They headed down the crowded street, with Aiden looking over his shoulder every few seconds to make sure they weren't followed. If anyone was trying to track them, they'd have a hard time keeping up with the twists and turns they took through the alleyways. Another thirty minutes and they made it to the stone arch of the Grand Bazaar. For five centuries the first covered market in the world had sprawled over the city's center. During the Ottoman Empire, Aiden told her, the market had been a fire lookout tower guarded by hundreds of soldiers. Today, the one bored and overworked security guard barely noticed the people flowing in and out of the giant entrance.

Rachel sucked in a deep breath. "Here we go."

She and Aiden eased themselves into the bustle of people wearing heavy coats. Heads down, they passed the smooth-faced security guard without being stopped. Inside the arched and ornate halls of the market-place, the music of the tambur, lute, and an end-blown flute floated on the spice-scented air, creating an ambiance intended to put a person in the mood for parting with their money.

"This way." Aiden led her along one of the many wide concrete aisles lined with lighted display windows. Perfume, jewelry, exquisite vases, clothing, and vibrant splashes of color surrounded her. Shop sellers waited beside stacks of multi-colored fabric, beautiful pottery, and inter-esting artwork, each of them smiling and calling out to attract the atten-tion of potential customers.

The experience would have been one to check off her bucket list had she not been distracted by the nagging thought that coming here had been a mistake. That somehow, they'd been lured into a trap.

Aiden easily found the pastry shop he'd given Iceman as the location of their meeting. He took her elbow and drew her close to him as they headed toward the back of the room. There was no turning back now.

She secured a small table while Aiden ordered their coffees. All around her people passed, oblivious to the nerves twisting in Rachel's gut. Only a couple of men let their eyes move from their deep conversa-tion to the blonde sitting in the corner, but their assessment was brief and unimpressed. Everyone else ignored her. After all, she was a woman. She doubted she would be so easily dismissed if they knew she possessed knowledge of a virus that could forever alter their lives.

She folded her hands together to steady her nerves, then spotted a tall handsome man with a blond crewcut coming her way.

Iceman.

The adrenaline pumping through her veins turned to ice at the sight of him. He was broad shouldered, muscled, and very sure of himself. His blue eyes locked with hers. Rachel's heart rate doubled as he strode to their table.

The blond microbiologist waited for Aiden to set the coffees on the table, then embraced Aiden. "Hey." They gave each other glad-to-see-you slaps on the back, then released. "Man, you scared me to death when you dropped off the grid."

"You scared me when you didn't answer my calls or texts," Aiden shot back.

"Yeah, about that—"

"Look, once we get this virus under control, we'll work on our protocols so that the next time we dig up something big, we won't have a communication breakdown."

"Aiden." Rachel had joined their huddle unnoticed.

Iceman eyed her approvingly. "If this beauty is the brains behind what you've been up to, no wonder you've laid low."

"Leave it alone, Ice." Aiden indicated they all should sit. "This is Dr. Rachel Allen. An epidemiologist and viral researcher at Gaumond Labs."

"Aiden has always kept the best for himself," Iceman said, like he was joking. But the words had a knife-blade edge.

"Really?" She wrapped her hands around one of the warm cups to steady her nerves. "That's not been my experience at all." Hair rose on the back of her neck in defense of what she perceived to be a cut against the man she'd come to care for. No. She couldn't allow herself to think that way.

Aiden pushed one of the cups of *noisette* toward his friend. "Tell me what you know about what's happening in Tibet."

"It's bad. The disease is spreading rapidly. We need that virus."

Rachel saw a flicker of hesitation in Aiden's eyes. "We've been doing some extensive testing."

"What kind of testing?"

"The kind that brings an end to an outbreak before it becomes a pandemic."

"Old man Zimmern helping you?"

"I'm here in Istanbul, aren't I?"

"Which is why I'm here now. I knew you'd go to him for help. We need to get the virus back to DC. This is bigger than the both of us.

Aiden shook his head. "It's too dangerous."

Rachel looked up. Two men dressed in black, the two men who'd chased them out of Gaumond Labs, were headed toward their table. "Aiden!" she whispered.

Aiden's gaze darted to where she'd nodded then back to Iceman. "You were followed?"

"It's not possible."

The men were coming closer, their hands going to the guns tucked inside their jackets.

Rachel flipped the table as one of the men in black shouted at them. Hot coffee spilled into Iceman's lap. "Run!" she screamed as she grabbed Aiden's hand.

FIFTEEN

Aiden jumped to his feet. Shots rang out and the glass pastry counter exploded. He pulled Rachel through the people scattering for cover.

"This way!" he shouted, as the three of them ran out the back door and turned into the crowded walkways of the market, trying to disappear into the crowd. He'd been certain they hadn't been followed to meet Iceman, but someone had tracked them down. Or had it been Iceman who'd given them away? He'd heard someone call out Iceman's name — Calum — or had he just imagined it?

At the moment, the only thing that mattered was that someone had found them. He guided them through a maze of narrow avenues and streets beneath the covered marketplace, his mind on only one thing. They had to lead whoever was after them away from Charlie and the virus.

They weaved in and out of haggling shoppers and sellers and through the crowded passageways lined with small shops selling everything from jewelry to furniture to leather goods and every kind of trinket in between. Iceman plowed into a container of rolled carpets, scattering them across the floor. Someone shouted. Aiden gripped Rachel's hand tighter, dodging around a group of tourists. He glanced behind them as they took another right then ran out of one of the exits. Once outside, he glanced behind them again. He couldn't see the men who'd come after them, but that didn't mean they weren't there.

"Come on!" He hurried down the narrow one-way pedestrian streets until he found a small alcove with a painted doorway. He tucked Rachel against the wall and squeezed in to make room for Iceman. Aiden's heart pounded as he glanced down the street sprinkled with people casually going on about their lives, but there was still no sign of the men he recognized as the same men who'd chased him and Rachel through DC.

He gripped Rachel's elbow. "You okay?"

Rachel nodded. "I think we lost them."

"I think so too, but I need to talk to Charlie." Aiden pulled out his phone, his frustration mounting when the old man didn't answer.

"Here's what I don't understand," Rachel huffed, still trying to catch her breath. "If they want the virus, why are they shooting at us? Doesn't that seem counterproductive?"

Aiden turned to Iceman, still alert for signs of the armed men dressed in black. "Do you know who they are?"

"Man, I'm as clueless as you are."

"They called your name."

A sick feeling washed through Aiden as his mind forced him to go to a place he'd been avoiding. He, Rachel, and Charlie had hashed over the possibility that it had been someone on the inside who was involved in stealing the information. But surely it wasn't Ice. They'd been best friends in college. Aiden had helped get him a job in his father's company. He'd trust him with his life. But something wasn't adding up.

"Ice?"

"I don't know. They must have followed me. I'm sorry. I tried to be careful."

Something about his friend's response seemed off. Aiden wasn't buying his excuses. "You know who they are, don't you?"

"Doesn't take a rocket scientist to figure out it has to be someone after the virus."

"Yes, but you said you had information on who was behind this."

"I do, but not here." He glanced down the street. "We need to go somewhere safe. Somewhere private." Iceman's phone dinged. He ignored it. "Let's go." He was nervous. On edge. They all were. But it was more than that.

Aiden caught a flicker of panic in Iceman's eyes. "Why are you really here?"

"I already told you. I figured you'd come here to see Charlie—"

"Ice. . .We've known each other for years." Aiden's gaze cut from his friend to the crowded street, then back to his friend. "What have you done? They were shooting at you. They called *your* name."

Iceman's jaw tensed. His brow beaded with sweat.

"Just tell me," Aiden said.

"I'm in trouble." Iceman pressed his back against the doorway. "I'm sorry, okay? I never meant for things to go this far, but I needed money, and they offered me a deal if I could get them the virus, but then. . .then you took off with it, and everything changed."

"We weren't supposed to be at the lab, right?"

Iceman nodded. "You were supposed to think it was just a robbery."

"Tell me what happened," Aiden demanded. "From the beginning."

"I got an email. They were interested in buying the virus. Somehow they knew about my gambling debts."

"So they blackmailed you?"

"Apparently, I was the perfect mark."

"Why didn't you come to me?"

"I'm sorry, man." Iceman's chest heaved as he took in a breath. "You've always had everything you wanted. But I don't. I needed the money and—"

"You sold us out." Aiden couldn't hold back his disappointment. "Everything we've worked for."

"They made me an offer I couldn't refuse. If you were in my position—"

"I wouldn't have compromised this mission or my ethics." Aiden rubbed the back of his neck, struggling to take in what Ice was saying. Trying to push aside the feelings of betrayal. "Haven't I always helped you?"

"Comes a time when a man has to stand on his own two feet. I'm tired of being your charity case."

"Charity?" Aiden shook his head. "Ice, I thought we were friends. Friends don't sell each other out."

"Their offer would have set me up for a very long time but—"

"But you didn't know how to find Charlie, right?"

"I'm sorry, Aiden. I need that virus."

"I trusted you. I've always trusted you like a brother." Anger and betrayal flooded through him, but those emotions weren't going to change the situation. "Who are they?"

"An interested party. Someone who knows about the virus."

"Whoever was intercepting our communications, right?"

Iceman nodded.

"In the wrong hands this virus can be turned into a bioweapon." Rachel spoke up for the first time. "Surely you knew that."

"It's too late to stop them," Iceman said. "And if I don't get them what they want, somebody else will."

"I still don't understand why they were shooting at you if you're supposed to lead them to the virus," Rachel said.

Iceman's gaze shifted to the gray cobblestone. "I got a second offer. A better offer."

"Wait a minute," Aiden said. "What are you saying?"

"It was stupid, I know. I really am sorry."

"Sorry you made the deal, or sorry they're after you now?"

"About everything," Iceman confessed.

"We'll settle this later. Let's go." Aiden pressed close to Rachel, his mind whirring as they jostled through the crowded street leading toward the ferry terminal, hoping they blended into the crowd. He didn't know how long he could stall, but hopefully it would be long enough for Charlie to realize he needed to pack up and head for the rendezvous point. Ten minutes later, he checked his phone for a message from Charlie.

Still no response.

They boarded the ferry and headed to the upper deck. Iceman guided them to the rail where all three of them watched as people boarded. There was still no sign of the men who'd chased them through the bazaar. As far as Aiden could tell, they'd lost their tail. But not hearing from Charlie had his anxiety rising. They couldn't go back to the apartment. Not if there was any chance they were being followed. And he couldn't trust Iceman. Which left them where?

Rachel sat on one of the wooden benches, staring out at the gulls diving alongside the boat. Historical minarets and the distinctive domes of the mosques and houses lined either shore as the ferry sailed from the European side of the city back to the Asian side. Feelings of protection tugged at Aiden's heart. The confinement of the lab and Charlie's apartment had given him the illusion that he was keeping Rachel safe. He never should have brought her with him today. Never should have brought her to Istanbul. But he'd never regret the time they'd spent together.

Iceman stepped up next to him at the railing. "I really am sorry."

"Prove it."

"I have information on who these guys are. If I give it to you, maybe we can stop this. Your father has connections. He'll know what to do."

"And what happens to you?"

"We use Ballinger resources to help me disappear."

Aiden frowned. He couldn't believe they were even having this conversation. "You've clearly made enemies. My dad's not a fan of making enemies."

"What are you suggesting? That I turn myself in?"

"If you don't, I will."

"You've always been so perfect. Playing by the rules."

Aidan caught the bitterness in his voice. How had it come to this? How had he not seen this coming? "What's the name of your contact?"

Iceman hesitated before answering. "He goes by the Titan. He contacted me via a text."

"Do you have the number?"

"I'm broke, not stupid. I kept all of our correspondence for insurance."

"I believe you're brilliant. That's what makes this so disappointing." Aiden studied his friend's face. On the surface Ice was handsome, tan, and capable of having the world on a string. How had he missed the broken thinking behind that perfect face? "Forward me everything you have. I have someone who might be able to help find out who's behind this."

Iceman pulled out his phone and forwarded the information. "Does this mean you'll help me disappear—"

"I need to think about that."

"Fine. I understand."

"Iceman."

"Forget it. You don't owe me anything." Iceman tugged on the bottom of his jacket. "I'm going to get some tea, but don't worry. I'm not going anywhere."

Aiden watched his friend walk away, then went to join Rachel on the bench, burying his feelings for the moment. "You warm enough? They have hot drinks downstairs."

"You trust that he's not slipped away to secretly let them know where to find us?"

Aiden shrugged. "I hope not. Your instincts were right. I wish I had listened."

"I'm sorry."

"I always saw him as a brother, and now. . .How could I have missed the resentment he's always felt toward me?"

"As hard as it is, sometimes nothing you do is enough for some people."

"That's not an easy thing to live with."

"Do you think he's telling the truth?"

Aiden pulled out his phone. "He sent me his correspondence with the buyer. I'll send it to my dad. I'm hoping he'll be able to help."

"What about Charlie?"

"We can't go back to the lab. We can't take the chance they could track us. All I can do is keep trying to contact him."

"And in the meantime?"

"I guess we find a place to stay under the radar."

"Charlie's almost done with the cloning. I think it's time we enlisted the CDC or WHO."

He nodded. Knew she was right. She looked up at him, eyes wide, lips pursed slightly. He suppressed the desire to kiss her again. Charlie was wrong. No matter what he did, she was never going to see him as just a normal guy. Just like Iceman. And there was nothing he could do to change who he was. They'd figure out how to get out of this mess they were in, and then she'd walk away.

A shot fired, jerking his attention away from his thoughts. They jumped up and headed toward the end of the ferry as it approached the shoreline. A commotion had broken out on the lower deck.

Rachel grabbed his arm. "Aiden. . ."

Passengers were screaming and running toward the railing as the ferry eased up to the dock. People on shore shouted. Someone had fallen overboard. A smaller boat sped away from the ferry. Shouts intensified as Aiden caught sight of Iceman's lifeless body bobbing in the water.

SIXTEEN

Aiden started for the water. "Ice!"

"No!" Rachel grabbed Aiden's arm and pulled him back from climbing over the rail, her gaze darting to find the person who'd fired that shot.

"I've got to help him—"

"Whoever shot Iceman must know we didn't give him the virus. They'll come for us next, Aiden." She hated the tangle of betrayal and unanswered questions swirling in Aiden's eyes. "We've got to protect Charlie and the virus."

He stared at her as if he needed to sit down with a hot cup of *noisette* and make sense out of this before he could move. But this was an equation more complicated than any they'd solved together this week. Waiting for a clear-cut answer was a luxury they didn't have.

She pulled him away from the dark, choppy water splashing against the dock. "Now, Aiden! We have to go now!"

Hand in hand, they snaked their way through the crowd gathering at the pier's edge to see what had happened. With each step, she felt Aiden's resistance to accepting the ugly truth lessen. They may never know the who, what, or why of Iceman's decision to sell out his longtime friend. Distant sirens drew closer.

"We've got to disappear before the police get here," Aiden said, his eyes suddenly clear and focused.

"Maybe it's time to get help."

"Who are we supposed to trust here?" Aiden's adrenaline and self-preservation had kicked in and he reclaimed the lead. "They find Charlie and this is not going to end pretty." He nodded toward the bus stop. "Come on."

They climbed aboard the next bus. Aiden led Rachel to the only empty seat. He stood beside her and held on to the overhead rail.

"Where are we going?"

"Somewhere off the grid until we can get ahold of Charlie," he said. "We'll get off at the next stop." He leaned down and whispered, "Once we're clear of all these prying eyes, you call Charlie and let him know what's up. I'll make sure we aren't being followed."

Rachel nodded, pulled her phone out, and mentally rehearsed the number she'd memorized for Charlie and hoped her hands weren't too shaky to dial.

"If we get separated, or if anything happens to me, I want you to go to the Kadiköy Rihtim Otel."

"The Kadiköy Rihtim Otel," she repeated.

"Go there and call my dad."

Another number, along with the number of Aiden's burner phone, that she'd been expected to memorize. The idea that either of them could suffer Iceman's fate was a possibility she did not want to think about.

"Aiden—"

He took her hand and gave it a reassuring squeeze. "You can do this, okay?"

"This city is a maze."

"It's near the water, and anyone should be able to give you directions." The bus screeched to a stop. "Let's go."

Rachel inched past Aiden and exited first into a cold, light mist making the street slick beneath her running shoes.

Aiden's phone dinged.

"Give me a sec," Aiden said, grabbing for his phone. "It might be Charlie."

The crowd pushed her forward. She forced her way out of the throng of people toward the row of shops, then turned around.

Where was Aiden?

A strong arm hooked her around the waist. Her phone went flying.

"Don't make a scene." A gloved hand came from behind, showing her the weapon. She kicked and clawed against the strength dragging her away. The oblivious crowd closed in behind them the way sand fills a hole. Aiden would never find her now.

They rounded a corner, Rachel still struggling to get her footing. Tires screeched, and a gruff voice ordered, "Get in."

The man holding her captive slid back the van's door and shoved her inside. He jumped in after her and slammed the door before she could scramble out.

He caught her arm then hurled her against the solid wall panels. "Settle down, or this could get worse." He raised his gun and pointed it at her head. "Where's the virus?" His perfect English had the southern twang she recognized from the night she'd listened to him talk on his phone while she and Aiden hid in an alcove of Gaumond Labs. She was pretty sure the face glowering at her now belonged to the same guy she'd seen threatening Dr. Moreno on the lab's security video.

Fear, heavy as a jungle cat, pounced on her. If this man had caused the blood in her boss's office, and if he'd been the one to pull the trigger on Iceman, he'd have no qualms about hurting her.

"I don't know," she whispered. Which was true.

She had no idea how to get back to Charlie's apartment on her own, and even if she did, she hoped Charlie would have figured out by now that something was wrong and disappeared. They'd agreed that he would take the cloned virus and his early vaccine trials to Aiden's father if they didn't come back by a certain time. Without her phone, she could only guess about how much time she and Aiden had lost running from these guys and their guns.

Where was Aiden? Had he seen what happened to her? Had they gotten him too? Rachel tried to choke back the panic rising in her throat. Her screams would never be heard over the roar of the van's motor.

"Check her for a phone," the driver ordered over his shoulder.

"I lost it." Rachel said, pushing her back against the panel in an effort to put as much distance as she could between her and these horrible men. "You owe me a new one, by the way."

"Shut up." The man raised the gun as if he intended to hit her. "You'll wish you'd helped us."

"I really don't know what you're talking about," she offered in hopes of finding out who these men were and why they were after the virus. "Explain it to me."

"You'll help." The man with the gun pulled out his phone and snapped her picture. "Or your brother and his family will suffer." He stuffed his phone back into his pocket then told the driver to return to base and dump the van.

Not Josiah. She didn't dare speak his name, although they probably already knew it and where to find him. Keeping them safe was on her.

Rachel moved her head slowly, hoping for a better view out the windshield. She needed to keep track of where she was so that if she got a chance to get away, she wouldn't waste time wandering around aimlessly. She tried to spot some landmarks as they flew down the narrow streets, but each tall apartment building and sidewalk market booth they passed looked just like the last.

The van made a sharp right then an abrupt stop that sent Rachel into a face-first sprawl. Her abductor grabbed her arm, yanked her to her feet, then jammed the gun barrel into her side. "If you try to run, it'll be the last thing you ever do."

He jumped from the van then reached in and pulled her out onto a street teeming with shops, vendors, and pedestrians. Gun poking hard against her heaving ribs, he led her toward a man selling candy. The dark-haired vendor, dressed in the little red hat and black coat of an old-time organ grinder, was making Turkish taffy in a round metal tray separated into different compartments. Rachel could smell the ground fruit flavored with mint, hibiscus, cinnamon, and cloves. The vendor saw them and immediately began to stir the sticky substances kept warm by a small flame beneath the tray. He quickly spun the hot silky taffy around a stick, gave it a squeeze of lemon, and offered it for sale.

Someone on a motorbike honked then zipped around when they didn't get out of the street. The man with the gun in Rachel's side pushed her past the vendor with a grunt. He shoved her through the outer door to the apartment building then up a flight of stairs and down a long hall. They stopped outside a door numbered 202.

He fished a key from his pocket. "Unlock it."

"Why are we here?"

"Better hope someone cares enough about you to be asking the same thing, beautiful."

Hands shaking, Rachel managed to comply. He reached around her, turned the knob, and shoved her inside. The space was dark and smelled of stale cigarette smoke and moldy carpet. He flipped on the light, a single bulb that hung in the middle of a room furnished with a table and two chairs and nothing else. He dragged her to the table and plopped her down in one of the chairs. Before she could ask more questions, he took zip ties from his pocket, wrapped her arms around the back of the chair, and tied her wrists.

"I need to use the restroom," she finally managed.

"Not until we get some answers."

Rachel clamped her lips. She was not giving up Charlie's location, and she sure wasn't giving up the virus.

She heard heavy footsteps on the stairs and soon learned they belonged to the driver. Both men stood over her, but only the one who'd grabbed her spoke. "I'll ask you one more time, where's the virus?"

"I don't know what you're talking about."

He smiled then slowly reached inside his jacket and pulled out a torn piece of paper. "Maybe this will jog your memory." The photograph he showed her was the one someone had taken from her apartment. Josiah, Camilla, and little Emma. "Tell us where you left the virus, or I make a call and someone in California will pay a little visit to your brother and his pretty little family."

Rachel's stomach leapt to her throat, but she kept her face poker straight, a technique she'd perfected from years of trying not to laugh at her brother's jokes. "I'm not saying anything until you let me use the restroom."

The silent one nodded to the man who'd taken a great deal of pleasure in tying her up. He slid his gun into his belt then pulled a knife from his pocket and opened the blade. With a sigh, he slit the plastic tie on her wrists. "Try anything, and I'll shoot you."

Rachel lifted her chin and walked to the tiny bathroom. She ignored the men's glares and closed the door. She leaned against the sink and tried to think what to do. On the other side of the door she could hear the men talking about how they hoped nabbing a hostage to use as leverage would make up for having to eliminate Iceman.

"Boss don't like when we don't follow orders," the man with the southern accent said.

Something fluttered in Rachel's peripheral vision. She turned toward the small window where a pigeon had landed. She stood on the stool and peered through the grimy glass. It was at least a ten-foot drop to the sidewalk below. The fall could break her leg. But from the snatches of conversation, worse would happen to her if she stayed here. Coughing as loud as she could to cover her moves, she checked to see if the window would open.

Thank the Lord, it did.

She flushed the toilet, screwed open both sink taps until they ran loud and hard, then shoved the window as wide as it would go. Palming the ledge, she heaved herself up and wiggled until she was out on a narrow ledge. She grabbed hold of a piece of guttering, prayed it would hold, then eased her feet over the edge. Dangling several feet above the ground, she considered the foolishness of this plan.

A head of dark hair thrust through the window above her. "I'll kill you."

Without hesitation, she dropped. Her foot struck the tray of hot candy and sent it rolling down the street. The vendor took off after it as she hit the sidewalk with a jarring thud. Scrambling to her feet, she started running down the crowded street, thankful she hadn't sprained anything. Where she went, didn't matter at this point. She'd get as far from here as possible, then ask someone for directions to the hotel, praying Aiden would be there waiting for her when she arrived.

She glanced behind her one last time and felt her breath catch as her captor stepped out onto the sidewalk and started running toward her.

SEVENTEEN

Aiden dropped into the red plush chair in the hotel lobby and stared at the blurry photo of Rachel on his phone. Panic slammed through him. He could see the terror and confusion in her eyes as she stared into the camera.

YOUR GIRLFRIEND FOR THE VIRUS.

KADIKOY MARKET.

30 MINUTES.

WILL CALL WITH FURTHER INSTRUCTIONS.

He grabbed his backpack and strode out of the hotel lobby, mind racing, as he tried to figure out how this had happened. His phone had gone off as they'd gotten off the bus, and he'd reached for it, thinking it was Charlie. One minute she'd been beside him, and then the next minute she'd been swallowed by the crowd. He'd tried to convince himself they'd just gotten separated. That there was nothing sinister about her disappearance. He'd walked up and down the street, glancing into shops, searching for her until he made it to the lobby of the hotel where he'd told her to meet him if they did get separated. But she hadn't been in any of the shops he'd scoured, and she wasn't answering her phone.

Now he knew why. The men who'd been chasing them had her and wanted to make a trade.

His heart pulsed in his throat. Iceman was dead. He couldn't get ahold of Charlie. And now Rachel was missing. He hadn't been able to protect anyone. A wet wind whipped around him as he headed toward the nearest bus stop. He'd already left a cryptic message for Charlie. Aiden had his own and Rachel's passports with him, but he wasn't going to leave the country without her or Charlie and the virus.

He pulled out his metro card as he boarded the bus then quickly found himself a seat, senses alert as he studied the passengers. No one seemed to be paying him any attention. He glanced out the window as the bus started moving. Rachel had talked to him about faith. How her father had died for his. How much faith did it take to turn a bad situation around? He'd spent his life trusting in his own might. What if stepping up his game wasn't going to be enough this time?

What if he couldn't stop those behind the evil?

What if he couldn't stop all of this from happening?

Because this situation seems impossible, God.

He got off the bus at the market, still battling the doubts. Rachel would love this neighborhood. The narrow pedestrian streets filled with coffee shops and restaurants. Rows of open stalls selling olives, spices, cheeses, fruits and vegetables, seafood, and jars and jars of pickled vegetables. It was a foodie paradise. Something he'd love to share with her.

He checked his phone, making sure he hadn't missed any calls. Thirty-six minutes had passed since he'd received the message.

Why hadn't they contacted him?

He shoved his hands into his pockets and started walking down one of the streets, searching for any sign of Rachel. Would they bring her out into the open, crowded market? More than likely whoever had grabbed Rachel wasn't going to bring her here. But then, where was she? A shiver slid up his spine as he glanced behind him. Were they watching him? Making sure he hadn't gone against their instructions and called the authorities? Or had something happened to her?

His gut churned as he breathed in the smell of fresh shellfish on ice. A black and white cat, searching for scraps, scurried past him. He checked his phone again. Another ten minutes had passed. Guilt pressed through him as he scanned the crowd. This wasn't something he could handle on his own. None of this was. He pulled out his phone again and dialed the familiar number.

"Dad?"

"Aiden. . .Where are you?"

"They have Rachel. They want to make an exchange—"

"Slow down and tell me what's going on."

"Whoever's after the virus. . .they found us." Aiden ducked beneath an awning and out of the rain that was starting to come down harder. "We met Iceman at the Grand Bazaar this morning, but he's dead, Dad."

"Dead? What happened?"

"He sold us out. We need to know who hired him."

"I got the messages you sent, and I'm working with someone, but it's going to take time to track who's behind all of this."

"And the security footage? Have you ID'd anyone yet?"

"Not yet. But I'm working with Moreno, and we've brought in Ellis Carter—"

"Wait a minute. We thought Moreno was dead. There was blood in his office and we saw a body on the news."

"That was one of the security guards. Moreno got roughed up, but he's okay."

"And you think we can trust Carter?" Aiden tried to downplay the panic in his voice, but knew he wasn't succeeding.

"I realize we don't have a lot of options, but we can't just sit on that virus indefinitely. Once the CDC and WHO get wind of what's happening in Tibet, we're going to have to have a pretty solid explanation in place."

"What am I supposed to do in the meantime? I can't make the trade, but I can't let anything happen to Rachel either." Someone bumped into him, and he felt his heart race. He turned and searched the crowd behind him. It was just a kid running to his mom. He needed to calm down. Panicking wasn't going to help him find her. It was only going to cloud his judgment.

"Where's Charlie?" his dad asked.

"I haven't been able to contact him, and I'm worried. If they can send me texts, I'm afraid they can find Charlie. Maybe they already have."

"What did they tell you?"

"To meet them at the Kadakoy market for further instructions, but it's been almost an hour and I haven't heard from them."

"I'm not sure what I can do from here."

"I know." Aiden rubbed the back of his neck, willing the tension to go away. "I never should have left DC."

"You did the only thing you could have at the moment. More than likely that virus would be well beyond our reach if you hadn't moved as fast as you did."

"Maybe, but people are dead, with the potential of things getting worse. I'm running out of options."

"I have a connection I can call. See if we can get you some help in finding her. And Aiden, I understand why you left DC, but there are some who are going to question your choice of collaborators."

"Like who?"

"I'm just. . .I'm worried you're being played."

Aiden's jaw tensed. "By Rachel?"

"I'll be honest, Son, the thought crossed my mind."

"Rachel isn't behind this. Trust me."

"Then how did they find you on the island?"

"I don't know, but whoever's behind this has to be well funded."

"True, but how well do you know her? Really know her?"

"Dad—"

"Just be careful. And don't let your emotions blind you into not seeing what's really going on."

Aiden's phone beeped and he glanced at the screen. "Dad, let me get back to you. I've got another call coming through."

He accepted the call.

"Aiden?"

"Rachel?" His heart froze in his chest as he looked around. "Rachel, are you okay?"

"I managed to get away from them, but they followed me. I think I lost them, but I'm not sure."

"I got a message from them. They're trying to make an exchange for the virus."

"I know."

"Where are you?"

"I'm. . .I'm at the Volley Hotel. The guy at the front desk let me use his phone to call you."

"Are you safe?"

"I don't know if I'll ever be safe again, Aiden. I'm scared. These guys —whoever they are—they know where my brother lives."

He knew what she was thinking. Shepherd and Iceman were dead. If they weren't careful, they were going to be next.

"I want you to stay where you are. Get out of sight. I'll be there as soon as I can."

He stepped back out into the rain. He couldn't dismiss the possibility this was some kind of trap. But neither was he surprised she'd managed to escape. He'd seen her resilience and willingness to do what was hard. This time, he flagged down a yellow taxicab. He should call and get the police involved, but there was no time to explain the situation. He'd tried so hard to keep Rachel and Charlie safe. He couldn't give up now.

Fifteen minutes later, the taxi pulled up in front of the hotel. Aiden started to slip the man the fare amount with a tip, when something caught his attention. A couple was heading for another taxi.

Rachel.

"Pull in next to the front of that car," Aiden ordered, "then wait for me."

"I can't—"

He squeezed the man's shoulder. "I'll make it worth your wait."

There was no time to make a plan. Aiden jumped out of the car and ran toward the other taxi. He skidded across the hood of the vehicle then came down hard on the man's side, tackling him to the ground. The gun the man was holding clattered on the cobblestones as Aiden fought to pin him to the ground.

"Grab it, Rachel."

Rachel picked up the gun and pointed it at the man. "Don't move."

Aiden stood and pressed his foot against the man's back. "I'd do what she said if I were you."

Aiden glanced at the growing crowd around them. He shouted at the valet to make sure the man didn't move until the police arrived and motioned for Rachel to give him the weapon.

He grabbed her hand. "We need to get out of here. Now."

Aiden pulled her toward the taxi, got them inside, and shouted at the driver, "Go. . .go. . .go."

Their driver pulled into traffic. "Where do you want me to go?"

"Just drive." Aiden pulled her into his arms "Are you okay?"

"I've had better days." She leaned against him, her body shaking.

He needed to plan their next step, but she was safe and alive. That was all he could think about for the moment. "I'm sorry," he said, looking down at her. "Sorry I dragged you into this. Sorry I lost you."

"Stop." She put a finger to his lips. "Coming with you was my decision."

"I'd say it was mainly because you didn't want to stay with my mom."

A hint of a smile crossed her lips. "You're cuter."

It was all he could do not to kiss her right there, but they weren't out of the woods yet. "So what happened?"

"I don't know. I thought I'd lost the guy, but I was wrong. He walked into the hotel and saw me. Came up to me with a gun. Told me to be quiet, or he'd shoot someone in the room." A streetlight caught the fear in her expression. "It was the same man who grabbed me at the bus stop. The same man from the security video in DC."

"I picked up his wallet." Aiden pulled out the ID he'd grabbed off the guy. "His name is Pete Jefferies. He's an American."

"Sent here to track down the virus."

"Probably hired. And paid to take out whoever stands in the way."

"They're not going to stop until they have the virus," Rachel whispered. "We need to get Charlie and leave the city now."

Aiden's phone went off again.

"It's Charlie. He's on the way to Ataturk. Let's get this virus back to DC."

EIGHTEEN

Blue and red lights from half a dozen squad cars flashed on the darkened runway of the private airport just outside DC.

"What's going on, Aiden?" Rachel asked from the co-pilot's seat.

His father had told him there were going to be those who questioned his decision to leave the country with the virus, but he hadn't expected the authorities to get involved so soon. How did they even know he had it? Someone had told them, but who? They'd left to keep the virus safe from whoever was after it, not to exploit it. And he could prove he'd made the right choice.

"Only one way to find out." Aiden unbelted, helped Rachel from the co-pilot seat then shouldered the cooler bag with the cloned virus. He stepped off the plane, Rachel and Charlie following.

The moment the three of them were on the tarmac, someone shouted, "Hands in the air, now. All three of you."

Uniformed officers encircled them. Panic surged as he complied, but his mind was still trying to process what was happening.

His father stepped between officers with their guns raised.

"Dad. . .what's going on?"

His father held up his hand. "I'm sorry, Son, but we found evidence Rachel and Charlie have been behind the attempts to steal the virus."

"What? You can't be serious." Rachel's voice rose a frantic notch. "Aiden, tell them I've helped you keep the virus safe."

"That could be true," Aiden's father said. "Except you didn't need the actual virus, did you?" When his father assumed his all-business stance, it never ended well for whoever opposed him. "All you needed was its genomic instructions, and you could make it from scratch. And you have that now."

"No," Rachel argued. "We were trying to protect the virus. Someone is—"

"I'm sorry, Miss Allen," one of the officers said, stepping forward, "but we have evidence that confirms what Mr. Ballinger is saying. We're arresting you for possessing a regulated substance with intent to manufacture a bioweapon."

"You can't be serious." Rachel kept shaking her head and all Aiden could think was how badly he wanted her confusion to mean he'd not been betrayed again. That he'd not been blinded by her beauty and brains. That he wasn't a total failure when it came to character assessment.

"What evidence?" Charlie demanded.

The officer ignored his question and started reading Rachel and Charlie their rights.

"Dad. . .this is insane." Aiden tried to intervene, but he was motioned back. "I don't care what your evidence is, she's not involved. Neither of them is."

"Aiden, you've got to do something," Rachel pleaded. "Explain to them what happened."

He caught the terror in Rachel's eyes as one of the officers handcuffed her. This couldn't be happening. He'd promised to protect her, and now they were blaming her and Charlie for everything that had happened since the moment they'd met at that party.

"I'm sorry, Aiden." His father blocked his path as officers led Rachel and Charlie toward the squad cars. "You might be enamored with her, but you don't really know her."

"I know her well enough to trust her with my life."

"This is your problem, Son." His father picked a stray thread from the lapel of his tailor-made suit coat. "You've always trusted the wrong people. You knew Charlie was guilty, and yet you continued to protect him. I tried to warn you. And your mother and I never did like that scholarship boy you took up with in college."

"This is wrong, and you know it."

"Is it? They both have the knowledge and the skills to pull this off. They played you, Aiden."

The siren blipped as the car with Rachel and Charlie pulled away. Aiden dropped his hands to his sides. There was no way he'd been played by them. Was there?

He turned to his father. "What kind of evidence do you have?"

"Emails. Texts. We were able to retrieve them off our servers at the lab. Burner phones and cash in her apartment. They'd been meeting with buyers with the intent of selling to a third party."

He wouldn't believe it. "How can this be? Charlie didn't even know I was coming to Istanbul. And Rachel had never met Charlie, not until I took her to his little backstreet lab. They're being framed, Dad."

"I wish you were right, Son, but this is what our investigation uncovered."

"And you turned all the evidence over to the authorities?"

"I couldn't let you throw away your life. There's a lot at stake here."

"What am I supposed to do?"

"Take the virus." He nodded toward a shiny black SUV. "Dr. Moreno and a deputy director from the CDC are waiting in the car. The three of you will go straight to the lab. We need to ensure whatever you have in that cooler never gets into the wrong hands."

"What are you going to do?"

"I'll be there soon. I've been asked to finish giving my statement. They'll want to talk to you next."

"This isn't right, Dad." He pulled out his phone. "I'm getting them a lawyer—"

"I already called someone, but you're not responsible for them. We'll make sure the entire truth comes out, but for now, your priority is securing the virus. I'll have your things delivered for you and meet you there."

Numbness spread through Aiden as he headed for the black SUV where he found Moreno in the driver's seat and the deputy director in the front passenger seat. He placed the virus cooler on the floor then climbed in behind them.

"Welcome back," Moreno said. "Though I'm guessing this isn't the ticker-tape parade you were expecting."

"No, it's not."

"This is Daniel Faraday with the CDC," Moreno said, making introductions. "This is Aiden Ballinger."

Aiden snapped on his seat belt as Moreno shifted into Drive then started toward the exit. "It's good to meet you, but I can't help but wonder why I'm coming with you and the virus instead of heading to a holding cell?"

"We never found any connection to you in the evidence," Faraday said.

"But Moreno, you know Rachel," Aiden countered. "You don't really believe she's guilty, do you?"

"I don't want to, but I've seen what they found. She had opportunity. . .motive. The police found cash stashed in her apartment. More than her annual salary."

Aiden pinched the bridge of his nose as a wave of exhaustion flooded through him. "I don't care what the evidence is, I still don't believe it."

"It's hard for me to see her involved in something like this too," Moreno said. "But according to her financials she has quite a bit of education debt."

"Her parents were missionaries. She had to take out loans to pay her own way." Aiden leaned back against the seat, wishing he could ignore the heavy feelings of betrayal. What if his father was right? How well did he really know Rachel? She was the one who'd claimed to be a missionary kid. He'd taken her at her word.

The thought that his father was right and he'd allowed this beautiful girl to play him with the same story of growing up poor Iceman had told him made him sick to his stomach on the one hand. Mad as a hornet on the other.

No. It simply wasn't possible. They'd spent hours talking about life and work and faith, and when she'd kissed him, he let his mind dare consider the possibility of something more than friendship with her. His gut clenched at the thought that he'd imagined the fierce connection between them. But then again, Iceman had betrayed him. Something he never would have imagined. Had he totally misread Rachel as well?

Aiden's head pounded and his body screamed for sleep after all he'd been through, but he couldn't rest. Not yet. This was far bigger than his personal feelings. He, of all people, knew how high the stakes were. Until this virus was secure, his original fears of a worldwide pandemic in the wrong hands was still a possibility.

He stared out the window, the lights of the city blurring together. "This isn't the way to the lab."

"I just got a message from your father," Moreno said from the front seat. "There's been a change of plans. He's worried about the security of the virus. Worried there could be more inside people involved."

"So where are we going?" Aiden asked.

"Another high-security lab not too far south of here."

Aiden shifted in his seat, not sure he was comfortable with the change of plans, but all he could think about was what Charlie and Rachel were going through and what questions they were being asked. His phone rang and he snatched it out of his pocket.

"Aiden?"

Aiden's heart hammered at the sound of the private investigator's voice he'd hired.

"Don't let on it's me." Evan rushed on before Aiden had a chance to speak.

"M-mom," Aiden stuttered. "Is everything okay?"

"I saw on the news that Rachel and Charlie were arrested when you landed in DC. They're being set up."

Aiden hesitated. "I know."

"Do you have the virus?" Evan asked.

"Yes."

"Is Moreno with you?"

The uneasiness in Aiden's gut spread as he shifted his gaze to the front seat. "Yes. Why?"

"Charlie and Rachel were framed, and I have proof."

The news slammed through him.

"Be very careful what you say and do right now," Evan said. "The people behind this, including Moreno, are powerful and dangerous."

"What do you want me to do, Mom? Ask Joel and Teresa to meet us for dinner?"

"Don't let that virus out of your sight. I'm working on an extraction plan."

"Look, Joel and I are kind of busy tonight. I'll come see you as soon as I can." Aiden dropped the phone into his lap, his looming paranoia growing.

"That was your mom?" Moreno asked, taking the exit off the freeway.

"Yeah."

Moreno cut a glance at him through the rearview mirror. "Everything okay?"

"Yeah, she's just in town to do a little shopping. Trying to settle her nerves after what happened on the island and all."

Dr. Moreno glanced in the mirror and smiled. "Iris has always been a firm believer in retail therapy."

Questions surfaced in rapid procession. If he couldn't trust Moreno, who was he supposed to trust? And how was he supposed to stop this? Was the deputy director, if that's who the man in the passenger seat really was, in on this with Moreno?

There was no time to process his thoughts.

"Hang on!" Moreno slammed on the brakes and jerked on the steering wheel as a car zipped in front of them.

Aiden lunged forward and tried to brace himself, but his head slammed against the window and everything went black.

Aiden had no idea how much time had passed when he woke to shouting. He shook his head, trying to clear his vision. Their vehicle wasn't moving anymore, and his head was pounding. Someone opened his door then yanked him out of the vehicle and onto the pavement before grabbing something out of the back seat.

The virus.

Aiden rolled over onto his bruised shoulder, trying to focus, but his vision was still blurred. He stumbled to his feet, forcing himself to stand up. His head throbbed, but he had to get the virus. Had to stop whoever had ambushed them and was taking it. He glanced into the front seat of the vehicle. The deputy director wasn't moving and the driver's seat was vacant.

Where was Moreno?

Movement shifted his attention to the left.

He blinked again. "Moreno?"

The older man had the cooler slung over his shoulder and was running away from the vehicle. A car honked as Aiden started running down the sidewalk, but all he saw was the friend he used to trust. He quickened his steps until he was only trailing him by a few feet, then lunged forward, tackling him to the ground. Both men rolled onto the grassy strip. Moreno turned, slammed his fist into Aiden's rib cage, then grabbed for the cooler again. Moreno might have thirty pounds on him, but Aiden was younger, stronger and faster. Sirens whirled in the distance as he pinned Moreno's shoulders to the ground.

"Give it up, Moreno. It's over," Aiden huffed.

Moreno struggled to get up. "You have no idea what you've just stepped into."

Aiden pressed his knee into the man's back. "Unfortunately, I think I do."

"I saw him running with the virus." The deputy director stood huffing over them. "Are you okay?"

"Yes," Aiden pulled Moreno to his feet while feelings of betrayal swept through him. "But I just learned there's proof the doc here was behind all of this. Not Charlie and Rachel."

"I don't know where you're getting your so-called proof," Moreno argued, as three police cars surrounded them, "but whatever you have is nothing more than lies."

Aiden shook his head and nodded to one of the officers. "Get him out of here."

Aiden walked into his parents' primary residence in Bethesda after being checked out at the emergency room. He tried to fight the emotions consuming him, but the past few days had shaken him.

His father strode across the marble tile toward him. "Are you okay?"

"For the most part." He stopped in the middle of the foyer, his hand going automatically to his shoulder. "I still have a headache from the impact, and I'll be sore for a few days."

"Thankfully nothing was broken."

Just his faith in humanity.

He studied his father's expression, surprised. "What's going on? I was told Charlie and Rachel are here and they've both been cleared."

"Thanks to the evidence your private investigator dug up, they have been." His father shoved his hands into his pockets and dropped his gaze. "I'm sorry. I was wrong about her. About both of them."

"You were just following the evidence. None of this was your fault."

"I understand how betrayed you feel by Iceman. Joel Moreno and I grew up together."

Aiden hated seeing the disappointment on his father's face, but he felt the same way. He'd admired Dr. Moreno and had considered him a friend. This wasn't how he'd expected this to end.

"They would both like to see you," his father said, motioning toward the library.

Aiden headed toward the room his mother had recently redecorated with mahogany bookshelves and leather furniture with stacks of colored pillows and throws.

When Charlie saw Aiden, his weariness disappeared from his face and he leapt to his feet.

"Thank you." Tears glistened in the old man's eyes as Aiden pulled him into a hug. "For believing in me."

"I never stopped."

Charlie fiddled with the buttons on his sweater. "Because of what you did, I might get to bring my work out of hiding."

Aiden shot him a grin. "You wouldn't mind that too much, would you?"

"I might get used to it. . .eventually."

"It's going to happen. I promise."

"I hope you're right, but for now, you need to talk to Rachel."

Aiden glanced around the room. "Where is she?"

"Out on the back deck. And, Aiden. . .you need to tell her how you feel."

"Charlie, I'm not sure I can —"

"Don't give me your excuses." Charlie clasped his shoulder. "The girl's in love with you, and I'm pretty sure you feel the same way about her."

His heart quickened as he stepped through the French doors. Rachel was sitting curled up on the end of a cushioned loveseat with a thick blanket wrapped around her. Even with dark circles from lack of sleep and tangled hair, she was beautiful.

"Aren't you cold?" Aiden sat down beside her, wrapped an arm around her shaking shoulders, and pulled her close.

"I'm not sure I can feel anything anymore."

"I am so, so sorry this happened." Aiden brushed away a tear from her cheek.

"I'm honestly not sure how to process everything. They just kept asking me the same questions, over and over, and I had no way to defend myself, because I didn't know anything. I haven't felt that terrified since. . ." She let her gaze drift toward the trees and Aiden knew she was thinking back to the day when a little girl stumbled upon men murdering her father. How he wished he could erase her pain.

"It was all a setup to frame you and Charlie."

"By Dr. Moreno?"

Aiden nodded.

"But why? I just. . .I can't believe he would do this."

"I've known Joel my whole life. Teresa must be crushed. We're still putting everything together, but from what Evan discovered, Joel's been planning the sale to a buyer for a long time. He didn't count on us running into his hired guns and taking the virus with us."

"Why did he involve me with the testing of the virus?" she asked.

"I'm guessing it gave him proof someone else inside the lab knew about the virus if he needed a scapegoat."

Rachel shook her head. "But he couldn't have counted on me meeting up with you and ending up with Charlie?"

"No, but he was able to use that to his advantage."

"If you hadn't hired Evan, Dr. Moreno's plan might have worked."

"It's possible." Aiden looked out at the red crabapple trees hovering above the layer of white snow blanketing the yard. "When Dad told Joel about a change of labs, Joel realized he wouldn't have unlimited access. So he planned to make it look like an ambush and run with the virus."

"At least he didn't get the virus. I never imagined Moreno being behind all of this. He wasn't just a boss. I always saw him as a friend." She pulled the blanket closer around her neck. "I guess he thought the virus was worth the risk."

"There are going to be more questions that still need to be answered, but speaking of taking risks." Aiden drew in a deep breath. "I have a question for you."

Her eyes widened as she looked up at him. "Okay."

"What about us? Do you think we're worth the risk? You and me? Together?"

He felt her shoulders relax slightly as she nuzzled her head against his chest, but he didn't miss the smile forming on her lips. "You know I've never been much of a risk-taker."

"Someone wise once told me that sometimes you have to take a leap of faith and trust God to do the impossible with our lives."

Her smile broadened as snow started falling again. "Then maybe it's time we both take that leap."

NINETEEN

One month later

Steam, laced with the sickening sweet odor of hydrogen sulfide, rose from the hot springs surrounded by jagged, snow-capped Himalayas. Rachel stuffed her gloves in her coat pocket and took the hardboiled egg the guide had cooked for her by lowering a wire basket into the bubbling waters. She carried the egg to the stone ledge built around one of the world's most beautiful outdoor saunas. Her numb fingers greedily cupped the hot egg. Keeping frostbite at bay had been the only drawback of spending the last couple weeks in the cold, isolated landscape of the "roof of the world." The rest of the time she, Aiden, and Charlie had worked with local Tibetan authorities to help reduce the spread of the disease throughout the remote villages had been wonderful. In fact, it was as if the heavy sadness she'd carried for years had vanished in the thin air. And with the lifting of her grief, she could finally retrieve the memories of the happy time her family had spent on the mission field.

Her father had been so much like Charlie. Kind, brilliant, and energized by helping others. He'd tried to teach her how to obtain that same joy by instilling deep within her a respect for God, a love for all people, and an appreciation of the beauty of this world.

While she waited on Aiden and Charlie to get their eggs, Rachel surveyed the pool Aiden had promised they would visit on their way home. He'd said hundreds of these springs bubbled up through the mountain crags and that wherever there was human presence in Tibet, you would usually find a hot spring within a hundred meters of their residence.

The tourists were easy to spot. Whether they were young and back-packing through Tibet or elderly and hoping that the healing waters of this magical place would restore their vitality, they were all wearing swimwear. The villagers—men, women, and children who'd traveled by foot through the mountains—dressed more modestly. They filled small bowls with the warm water and took long drinks as if they expected the warmth to sustain them through the coming months of bitter cold.

"You'll freeze if you don't get in." Aiden popped a bite of his peeled egg into his mouth. "Come on, you've got to try it."

Rachel held her egg tight. "I didn't bring a swimsuit, and besides, if we don't leave soon, we'll miss tonight's virtual reporting to your father."

"Thought you were past following all the rules." Aiden peeled out of his coat and stripped down to his long johns and T-shirt, seemingly unaware of how his actions sent pinpricks of awareness coursing through her body. The sensations had been there since the moment they met, but these last few weeks of working side by side with this man had increased their frequency and power. It was almost as if some sort of previously-unknown-to-her virus cell had invaded her body and was multiplying at such a rapid pace she feared she would be overtaken.

"I've learned that not following the rules can lead to prison time." She smiled back at him, but she was only half joking. Being arrested had been worse than any of the scenarios she'd pre-planned in her head. "If it hadn't been for your father and Evan, I would have lost my career because I didn't follow the rules."

"You were set up, Rachel. Everyone knows that. The risks you took on behalf of medical science stopped a global pandemic. That's the kind of stuff that'll make it hard for me to keep you on my team. Every research facility in the world is already calling. You can write your own ticket." He pulled his shirt over his head, his bare chest heaving as he stood facing her. "But if you still need every *T* crossed and every *I* dotted before you can feel good about saving the world, then here's the first rule of fieldwork. . .improvisation." Lifting and toting all of the boxes and boxes of medical supplies and food Gaumond Labs had donated to the remote village had corded every muscle of his lean torso. "Evil never follows the rules. And I, for one, will do whatever it takes to keep evil from winning." He pointed at the egg in her hand and kicked off his hiking boots. "Last one in is a rotten egg."

He was right. Evil would have won if she'd fallen back on her safety net of needing to have all the facts and play it safe.

Wearing only his long johns, Aiden slid into the water. He let out a satisfied yelp then dropped down until he was shoulder deep. "You can't beat it," — his hands swirled the bubbling water back and forth — "God's idea of a hot tub."

Rachel's giggle turned a few wet heads, but she didn't care. "Not a bad analogy."

"My leap of faith paid off." Aiden stretched out his arms, fell back, and floated with his face pointed at the clouds the sunset was turning shades of gold and red. "I've seen some pretty convincing stuff since you tossed your hat into my little three-ringed circus."

"Like?"

He kept himself afloat with slow easy movements. "Like the containment of a prehistoric virus. Our safety. Your exoneration." He righted himself, dragged his hand over his wet face, then looked her square in the eye. "Meeting you." He held out his hand. "Come on. Trust me."

Heat flushed Rachel's cheeks. "If that water is hot enough to boil this egg" — she held it up — "what will it do to me?"

Aiden splashed water up at her. "Tibetans claim the springs can heal you of all that ails you."

"Nothing's ailing me."

"You seem a little wound up to me," Charlie said as he shuffled past her in his bare feet, wrinkled pants, no glasses, and for the first time since she'd met him, minus his sweater. "Life's short, Rachel. Let's live a little, shall we?"

Charlie did a cannonball into the pool and sent a warm shower that drenched Rachel's hair.

Rachel jumped back and used the towel draped around her parka to wipe her face. "Charlie Zimmern, you old devil."

Charlie chortled and paddled to the other side of the pool. He began to chat with the locals in their dialect, his fluency in languages another quirk that didn't surprise her.

"Well?" Aiden asked. "Are you gonna play it safe or live a little?"

Rachel dropped her wet towel and carefully placed her egg in the protective nest of fabric. She removed her parka, unlaced her boots, and pulled off her socks. She hesitated at the edge.

"You'll sink in those heavy pants." Aiden smiled.

She peeled down to the long johns she'd been wearing for the last week and stood before him, aware that he was looking at her as if he could see into the depths of her soul. Like he could see every flaw, every fear, every desire. . .and none of it frightened him. He wanted to be a part of her. All of her. And that was both exhilarating and terrifying.

He waved her forward, his grin opening the gate to her heart.

She took Aiden's hand. Secure in his grip, she stepped into the pool. The first step was slicker than she expected, and she tumbled into Aiden's wet chest. His hands immediately went to her waist, but when she tried to pull away, he held her close, the vapor from their breath forming one cloud.

For a moment the world stood still. The bad viruses lurking just below the ice or behind the locked door of some secret lab were far away. The evil people trying to create havoc and suffering for their own gain had all been justly dealt with. There wasn't even a sweaterless old man paddling around keeping a pleased eye on them. There was just the two of them standing with their arms around each other in a peaceful pool of warm bath water high in the oxygen-thin alpine zone.

Wrapped around each other, they drifted and played in the water. When Charlie finally waded over to them and announced he was getting out before he turned into a prune, it was the first time that Rachel noticed the flaming blaze of sunset had sunk, leaving the sky a dusky gray. Night would come quickly.

She didn't want this day to be over. In the morning, they would board a bus and ride to the train station. The construction of the railroad tracks had cut the travel time across China's provinces from six months to several days, but the grueling work had also unearthed the virus. Lives had been lost in the name of progress, Iceman included.

She reached up and pushed a wet strand from Aiden's forehead. "I'm glad the people of Tibet are equipped to deal with this virus until a vaccine is created. That the world is safer. That I met you."

Aiden hooked his arm around her waist. "Rachel, I—"

"Did you two lovebirds hear me?" Charlie's question echoed in the valley. "I'm getting out."

"Okay, Charlie," Rachel managed, her gaze locked with Aiden's and her heart pounding in her chest.

"Remember what we talked about, Aiden," Charlie said.

Rachel turned back to Aiden. "What did the two of you talk about?"

Aiden pulled her close. "Do you know the legend about how this hot spring was formed?"

"No," she whispered, unable to catch a deep breath. "But you're changing the subject."

"Dameiyong was the third daughter of Meili Snow Mountain. When Dameiyong arrived in this valley, she saw that the people suffered from pestilence. She was so sad she couldn't stop crying. Her tears became this hot spring, and when the sick came down from the slopes to investigate the strange steam rising from the valley, they were cured." Aiden turned her toward the tallest mountain, the peak where they'd spent days administering vaccines and medicines. "Your heart for the hurting is as beautiful as you."

She laced her hands with his. "I have my own confession. I think I'm in love with you."

"That's the riskiest thing I've ever heard you say, and I've seen you do some pretty brave stuff."

"I've come to realize that my dad didn't raise me to live cautiously. He lived every day with his heart open to whatever the Lord asked of him. Most of it was risky, but he did it anyway. His fearless dedication to the Lord cost him his life, but I know blessing others blessed him most of all. I want to live like that." Her heart clutched at the confession, not with fear but joy. "Life doesn't always play by the rules, isn't that what you said?"

Aiden cupped her face with both hands and wiped the tear that ran down her cheek with his thumb. "I can't promise I can completely cure all of your hurts, but I can promise that you won't regret letting yourself love and be loved." His lips met hers with a gentle touch that quickly flowed from exploration to an elevation higher than the plateau they were on.

She wrapped her arms around him and drew him close, mentally vowing to never play it safe again.

"There is one more thing," Aiden said, his lips close to hers. "Are you willing to take another risk?"

"What risk would that be?"

"I know this has all been a whirlwind, but will you marry me, Rachel Allen?"

She smiled. "Is that what you and Charlie talked about?"

"Forget about Charlie. This decision is all mine." He unclasped the leather bracelet Samuel had given him. "I don't have a ring, but this is worth more to me—"

"Yes. Definitely yes." She waited for him to slip the bracelet around her wrist then wrapped her arms around him. Over Aiden's shoulder she could see the rise of a new moon. "And the sooner the better, Aiden Ballinger."

EPILOGUE

He'd always hated Washington DC in the winter. He only came here when he was called in to clean up a mess. Like tonight. He raised the collar on his coat, put his gloved hands into his pockets, and leaned against the bridge railing. The lights of this despicable city shimmered on the surface of the Potomac River.

Footsteps approached, but he didn't turn around. Moreno had proven to be tougher to manipulate than planned, but that hadn't stopped things from moving forward. Undertakings of this magnitude required time and effort. And in this situation, it was the bigger picture that mattered. They were just going to have to be patient and convince the buyers to do the same.

"My payment's late."

"It will be in your account later today," he said, turning around. "What do you have for me?"

The other man hesitated. "Aiden just asked her to marry him."

"You sound worried."

There was a hesitation in the other man's voice. "I am."

"I'm listening."

The man blew out a sharp breath and stared across the water. "I'm not sure I want to do this anymore."

Anger bubbled in his gut, but he forced the ire down. Losing his temper wouldn't solve anything. "What are you talking about? Everything's going according to plan."

"I've taken a lot of risks and need to be compensated."

"If you ask me, you're already over-compensated."

"If I get caught. . ."

"You're worried because of Moreno?"

"If he talks—"

"I've made sure he won't. You don't have anything to worry about."

"He's facing twenty years in prison. He'll talk."

A sight-seeing tour boat passed in front of them. The glass-covered deck was filled with tourists gawking for a glimpse at the Washington Monument and Lincoln Memorial while feasting on a three-course meal. Dealing with problems, like the one standing in front of him, was becoming too frequent and time-consuming.

"You should have checked your conscience at the door before deciding to be a part of this. You know you can't just walk away. You're in far too deep."

"You don't understand. My wife keeps asking me questions. Why I keep coming home so late at night and working so many hours. She thinks I'm having an affair."

"This will all be over soon and you can take her on that around-the-world cruise you keep talking about."

"I'm not sure she'll want to go with me."

He tightened his fists at his sides. "I'm not much for making threats, but you knew what you were getting into when you signed up for this. We're now moving into stage three. This will work."

"And if they don't agree to help?"

"Do you really think that's going to be an issue? Considering the information we have on them?"

"No, but—"

He caught the other man's gaze as he fought to keep his voice calm. "I don't have time for your guilt. You're either in or out, but if you decide to walk away—"

"Are you threatening me?"

He wrapped his gloved hand around the small gun in his pocket. "I would hate for you to suffer the fate of Shepherd."

"Maybe you've forgotten that I'm not the only one with blood on my hands."

"I was hoping things wouldn't come to this, but if you're going to be a liability, if I can't trust you—"

"You can trust me. All I'm saying is, if I'm going to continue risking my life, I need to talk to the Titan."

"No one talks to the Titan."

"Please—"

He didn't wait for him to complete his sentence. The sound of the gunshot was muffled by the silencer. Seconds later, the man's lifeless body slid into the river.

He reholstered his gun and walked away. The fear of getting caught had long since passed.

Watch for Death Triangle
The next book in the Angels of Mercy Series

ACKNOWLEDGMENTS

We are always so grateful for our readers. Your enthusiastic support for our work keeps us at our computers from early in the morning until late at night.

Our early reading team is the best. Your sharp eyes and sharper insights help us polish the story until it shines. A special thanks to Ellen Tarver, Jana Leasure, Janet Johnson, Judy Gentry, Jane Thornton, Ian Acheson, and D.L. Wood. Your eagerness to help spread the word about this series is such an encouragement to us.

During this time of a real pandemic, the support and love of family and friends has become even more treasured. We've also acquired a greater appreciation for those who have been and continue to be on the medical frontlines of the world's battle to defeat Covid-19. Thank you doesn't seem sufficient, but we thank you and pray for your continued health and strength.

To the One who knows our future, no matter how bleak our present, we believe you hold us safely in Your hands. We give You, O Lord, all glory, honor, and praise.

A NOTE FROM LISA AND LYNNE

Dear Reader,

Thank you for reading *Lethal Outbreak*, Book 3 in our Agents of Mercy series. If you're new to our series, we want you to know that each book can be read on its own. But you'll be glad you've already read *Lethal Outbreak* because when you get to Book 4, *Death Triangle*, you'll see how the entire series is tied together by someone you met in this story. If you're new to our Agents of Mercy series, we recommend you go back and read *Ghost Heart* and *Port of Origin*, then finish up with *Death Triangle* that will release soon.

You can find out more about our work on our websites: www.lisaharriswrites.com and www.LynneGentry.com.

Lisa and Lynne

THE AGENTS OF MERCY SERIES

"GRIPPING, RIVETING, UNNERVING."

Thank you for investing in this nail-biting medical thriller. Read on to find out more about the series!

Ghost Heart
Port of Origin
Lethal Outbreak
Death Triangle

GHOST HEART: BOOK ONE

Thank you for investing in this nail-biting medical thriller. GHOST HEART is the story of how far two mothers will go to save their children. Don't miss this award nominated thriller. CLICK HERE to get your copy of book one today.

PROLOGUE AND CHAPTER ONE

GHOST HEART

According to legend, their kind could never die. When they grew old, they simply vanished from this world, like smoke from the cooking fire that snakes above the spindly baobab trees and slithers away.

But not all legends are true.

Or so Jeme prayed.

Squinting through the shimmering rays of the grueling African sun, Jeme balanced the bowl of dried beans on her head and pressed through the crowded marketplace. A maze of narrow paths twisted around her, each lined with dozens of sellers who sat in cramped wooden shops displaying wares on rickety tables.

The smell of curried meat roasting on the grills mingled with the pungent odor of dried fish baking in the late afternoon heat. Jeme's empty stomach roiled as she hurried past piles of tomatoes, peppers, oranges, and colorful bags of spices. If only she could escape the whispers competing with the buzz of the buyers and sellers. Whispers that spoke of the magical powers of albino blood spilled across the brown earth, and of potions that could bring untold wealth.

She stepped into a puddle left over from the late afternoon rains, barely noticing the mud oozing between her toes. In Makuru, fish and vegetables weren't the only things for sale.

There was a price for human flesh, promising the strongest magic.

A flash of red caught her eye then vanished behind one of the tin-roofed stalls. Jeme jerked around, her breath tangled in the fear that had long ago taken root. Her fingers pressed against the rough wood of the kiosk as her eyes searched for the hunters. If they trailed her to the home she shared with Mbui, Numa, and Zaina, they would uncover her secret.

Jeme willed her heart to stop its frantic pounding and slipped through the back entrance of the market. Without the cover of the pulsing throng, she would be easier to track. Nerves on high alert, she hurried down the dirt path that led to her compound.

Something snapped behind her.

A fleeting look revealed nothing more than a boy watching his herd of goats in the grassy field beyond the market. She fingered the charm around her neck. She couldn't be too careful.

She longed for Mbui's presence and his cunning way of making their path difficult to follow. Not so many months ago, her husband had walked her home from the market each evening to ensure her safety from those who believed in the legend. Then fever attacked him, and Mbui's strength left.

Doctors from the hospital in Dar es Salaam promised her husband a new heart and a new life, but two days ago the fever returned, hotter than ever. He was dying because of the curse. Today she'd called his doctor, begging her to come before she had to bury Mbui beneath the baobab tree.

A quick glance at the setting sun only added to her concern. There was still no sign of Dr. Kendall's plane.

Fifteen minutes passed before Jeme reached the end of the winding path. Uncertain whether or not she'd been followed, she crouched in the shadows edging the compound. She studied the home she'd grown to love. Mbui's once strong hands had built the three huts, with their thick thatched roofs and solid mud walls.

Everything looked the same as when she'd left before the sun had risen from its bed in the sky. Tattered pieces of laundry fluttered in the breeze. Chickens pecked the twig-swept yard. And their goat remained tethered to a sturdy papaya tree. There was no sign of her sister, but Numa rarely ventured into the sunlight.

Glancing over her shoulder, Jeme slipped from the dense foliage. Shooing chickens from her path, she quickly crossed the yard. She passed the hut she and Mbui shared and went straight to her sister's door. She stopped and stared at the crude wooden slab hanging slightly ajar.

She knocked. "Numa?"

Nothing.

Jeme knocked again, panic rising at her failure to rouse her sister's cheery response. She pressed on the door. It creaked open. A beam of light spilled onto the floor. She stepped across the threshold, letting her eyes adjust to the silent darkness.

"Numa?"

Jeme froze.

A skinned body lay in a pool of blood.

"Numa!" Jeme fell to the packed-dirt floor. "No!" Her legs refused to stand, so she crawled the short distance to her sister. Body trembling, she sought Numa's hands, but they were gone. Every limb was gone.

"No!" Her screams rose through the thatched roof.

Jeme pounded the earth, cursing the ancestors who had forsaken her sister. Tears streamed down her cheeks as the sobs shook her chest.

Zaina!

Terror sliced through Jeme with the force of Mbui's sugarcane machete. Where was her daughter?

Jeme jumped up, screaming for the child she'd left in the care of her sister. She tripped over a pile of cooking pots, barely managing to keep her balance as she frantically searched the dark shadows of the room for signs of her baby.

"Zaina!"

Chest heaving, Jeme stopped in the center of the hut. She couldn't breathe. She couldn't think. She couldn't live without her child.

A soft cry broke through the stillness.

She turned to her sister's tiny bed, threw off the thin blanket, and shoved the mattress onto the floor. On top of the wooden bed slats, Zaina lay wrapped tightly in Numa's *kanga*.

Jeme pulled the crying infant toward her pounding chest and quickly quieted her with the offer of her swollen breast. Rocking back and forth, she glanced from the lifeless body of Numa to the door. What should she do? Because it wasn't her own dark skin the albino hunters were after.

Jeme caressed the soft, pale skin of her daughter's pinkish feet. Eventually, the blazing African sun would bake her child's delicate skin until it was thick and leathery. Blemishes would rise and mark Zaina's beautiful face like inky splotches on white paper—like Numa.

Jeme tucked her towheaded daughter deep into the faded cloth and tied her securely onto her back. She would not allow her own flesh and blood to become the hunted.

But if she stayed here, it was only a matter of time before human poachers found this cursed child.

December 11th, 9:34 AM EST

cincinnati, ohio

Catherine Taylor maneuvered her daughter's stroller around the redheaded toddler squatting amongst the Legos scattered on the gleaming waiting room floor. Although five years of weekly visits to the cardiologist had failed to make the jungle-themed office feel like home, joining other parents in their fight against similar heart defects had spawned a sense of family.

"Look, Kelsey." Catherine peered around the stroller cover. Blonde curls framed the angelic face of the underweight child holding a stuffed monkey in one hand and her soothing blanket in the other. Normal five-year-olds had given up their blankets by now, but the gap between Kelsey and normal children was growing wider by the day. "It's your friend, Timmy."

Kelsey's frail little arm extended the toy she'd requested in her Santa letter. "Want to see my new monkey?" When Kelsey asked why Santa had brought her gifts early and not her brother's, Catherine had told her it was because Santa's sleigh would be too full. The truth was, Christmas was two weeks away, and she couldn't bear it if Kelsey died before she opened her gifts.

"Let's see if Timmy is feeling better before we share." Catherine quickly wheeled the stroller wide as she eyed the small boy for any signs of last week's runny nose.

Susan, Timmy's mother, left her seat and wrapped a protective arm around her son. "He's not contagious." Desperate eyes, sunken in the haggard shell of former soccer-mom beauty, searched Catherine's for a bit of understanding. Understanding Catherine could no longer afford.

Everything in Dr. Finke's lobby had been specifically chosen so that it could be sterilized on a daily basis. But neither mother could deny what worried them most. The unseen microorganisms. Those microscopic missiles of death that traveled the airwaves seeking to destroy weakened targets like Kelsey and Timmy. Contracting a single germ that normal children shrugged off could kill their babies.

Catherine parked Kelsey in the far corner...just in case. "How did Timmy manage to shake that cold?"

Susan nervously tucked a strand of mahogany hair behind her ear. "Two rounds of antibiotics."

"Whatever it takes, right?" Catherine offered Susan the same hopeful, but useless smile other mothers had once offered her. The clock was ticking and antibiotics wouldn't slow it down.

She removed her fur-lined gloves and dropped them into the giant tote bag she lugged whenever forced to leave the house.

"I want out, Momma."

If only Kelsey could run and play. "Hang on, punkin." Catherine unzipped Kelsey's pink parka and freed her twig-like arms. Ugly purple tracks from endless blood tests scored the tender flesh between her daughter's wrists and elbows. Longing to kiss away the painful bruises, she folded Kelsey's arms across the labored rise and fall of her little chest. How much longer could her child endure this medical poking and prodding?

Kelsey whimpered, but didn't complain. "Can you turn me to the wall?"

All sorts of animals were hidden in the foliage of the wallpaper jungle scene. Kelsey tried to spot a new creature every time they came for a checkup. Last time, she'd found the monkey. His ability to leap from tree to tree had so entranced her, nothing would do until she had one of her own.

"Sure." Catherine checked her watch and felt her own heart lurch. She'd nearly missed the morning meds.

"Punkin, it's time for your special milk." Catherine scooped her daughter into her arms and sank into the nearest chair.

"But I want to show my monkey to the monkey on the wall," Kelsey protested.

"Take a drink for Momma, and I'll help you introduce your monkey to the monkey on the wall." She kissed the nest of curls nuzzled against her chest, drinking in the baby-shampoo scent of her sweet girl.

Digging into her tote bag, Catherine sorted through an assortment of Ziploc bags until she found the one with the Sippy cup. If she could cajole Kelsey into taking half an ounce of the milky supplement, then maybe they'd have a shot at keeping today's meds in her child's distended tummy.

She held the cup to her daughter's clamped lips. "Please. Just one sip."

"I'm tired." A fussy shake of Kelsey's head signaled the start of the cycle of absolute refusal.

Pain, combined with the disgusting taste of the medicine regime, always transformed her child's normally sunny disposition into a full-blown tantrum. Within moments of the exertion, the panting spells would begin. Afraid Kelsey could no longer tolerate the trauma, Catherine withdrew the cup. "Maybe later then." She snatched the night-night from the stroller and offered the silky-edged blanket to her snuffling child.

Kelsey accepted one of the few things that could soothe her and drew herself into a ball around its soft comfort. Seconds later, she drifted off to sleep.

Holding her dormant child tight, Catherine resisted the urge to check for the faint irregular beat of Kelsey's struggling heart.

How long did they have before the deformed organ gave up its battle?

Carefully, she returned her youngest to the stroller, relieved when she saw Kelsey take a breath. She stroked the damp curls away from her daughter's pale, oval face.

Nothing so perfect on the outside could possibly have something so wrong on the inside. A lie, she knew. But easier to swallow than the truth.

Scrubbing the untouched drinking cup with an antibacterial wipe, Catherine refused to give in to the panic knotting her gut. According to Brad, their daughter was a fighter, inheriting her stubborn streak from Catherine. Thank God. If Kelsey had been born with Brad's everything-will-work-out personality, her shriveled blue body would have never made it out of the preemie unit of Cincinnati's NICU.

Catherine sealed the cup in the Ziploc then stuffed it inside Kelsey's bag. Keeping Kelsey hydrated and medicated had become a vicious cycle of trying to stay on the clock. If she delayed forcing Kelsey's morning meds down her, the med schedule would be off for the entire day. She made a mental note to ask Dr. Finke to explain the feeding tube he'd mentioned last week. Maybe if Kelsey's meds could be pumped directly into her frail body, things would turn around. A desperate measure, but one she was more inclined to consider due to Kelsey's continued deterioration.

In an attempt to quiet the butterflies aloft in her stomach, Catherine picked up the same dog-eared parenting magazine she'd read every office visit for the last five years. Flipping the pages without actually reading a word, she watched Timmy quietly press together plastic blocks with older-child precision. Every week, he built imaginary cars he would probably never drive and lopsided castles he would never fill with his own children.

Catherine's eyes slid from the boy to his mother. Susan, perched on the edge of a green-leather seat, stared at Catherine's sleeping daughter. Susan teetered on the brink of a catastrophe similar to Catherine's, and from the pinched look on her face, she knew it. Any moment Susan's son could be lying listless in a stroller while other mothers looked on and thanked their lucky stars he was not their child.

In Susan's fearful gaze, Catherine saw what she'd been telling herself could not be true. Until a few weeks ago, Kelsey's limited play mimicked Timmy's. She'd play quietly with her baby doll, stopping every few minutes to fold herself into the squatting position. The pressure against her chest granted the swollen aorta of her boot-shaped heart a brief reprieve while forcing oxygen-deprived blood into hungry lungs.

Catherine adjusted Kelsey's blanket, her own heart sinking at her inability to rouse her daughter even a little.

Susan reached down and helped Timmy snap two Legos together. Envy, bitter as bile stung Catherine's tongue. Timmy still had a bit of rose in his cheeks. Catherine glanced at Kelsey's sleeping face and grimaced at the total void of color.

Terror clawed at her insides. Kelsey's worsening condition was not Susan's fault. The poor woman would soon have more troubles than any mother should ever have to bear.

"Is it someone's naptime?" Susan's attempt to sound upbeat fell flat.

Catherine stifled the urge to scream, her clenched sigh ruffling her stringy bangs in desperate need of a trim. "Twenty hours out of twenty-four."

Susan nodded, letting the snippy answer go unquestioned.

"Sorry, Susan...I..." Catherine closed the magazine and laid it on the table. Her friend didn't deserve the anger that boiled just below the steely exterior she worked to maintain. But try as she might, she couldn't shake the urge to hit someone. Even on those rare occasions when Brad put forth the extra effort to spell her, she couldn't escape the feeling that any moment she could blow.

Susan dismissed the apology with a wave. "Is she—" Her voice fragile as a brittle leaf. "—going to need a transplant?"

"We find out today."

Susan crossed the room and slipped into the chair beside Catherine. "I've been doing some research. On the Internet." She looked around the room as if it were bugged then quickly removed several printed pages from her purse and handed them to Catherine. "Just in case."

"What is this?"

"You can get a heart. If you have the money."

Trepidation rattled the papers in Catherine's hands. She quickly thumbed through them, trying to make sense of the printed words. She stopped on the page with a red, lopsided heart shaped map in the upper right hand corner. "What are you talking about?"

"Did your insurance grant preapproval?"

"Brad's checking on the hold up." Catherine glanced at the page again. This wasn't a heart logo. This was a map of Africa. Her stomach cartwheeled. "But we've bought a supplemental policy just in case."

"Good thing, because in the States, a new heart is going to cost over a million dollars."

"I know. I've checked the numbers."

"Well, in some countries"—Susan scanned the room again—"hearts are more...affordable."

Catherine stiffened, folded the papers, and handed them back to Susan. "I'm not looking for a clearance rack special to replace my daughter's heart."

"How long can you afford to wait?" Susan tilted her head in Kelsey's direction. When Catherine said nothing, Susan dropped the papers in Catherine's lap. "I'm just saying, I'd think about it if it were me." She squeezed Catherine's arm and then quietly retreated to her side of the waiting room.

Hands trembling, Catherine crammed the papers into her tote. How dare Susan claim to know how much time Kelsey had left. She couldn't know that any more than she could know about Africa. Just because the woman had googled something on the Internet didn't make it true.

So why would she believe Susan?

Catherine straightened her blouse. Kelsey had time. Lots of it. She dug around in the tote bag and fished out a Ziploc of bottles and pill canisters. Kelsey had to have those meds.

Catherine blocked the hum of Timmy's pretend cars, but Susan's tendered advice continued its assault upon everything she hoped was true. Dr. Finke was the best pediatric heart surgeon in Ohio. He'd fixed Kelsey before...twice. Catherine was counting on him to do it again.

Taking her baby to some dirty, foreign country so some witch doctor could wave a magic potion over her was out of the question. Who in their right mind would let some quack who probably flunked out of an American med school operate on their child in a primitive, third-world facility?

Catherine fumed while Susan let Timmy drive his Lego car over her face. Susan was crazy. Why hadn't she noticed the woman's desperation before? The truth hit Catherine like cold water in the face. Taking care of a sick child had dried up her own well of common sense.

Think. She had to calm down and think.

From the moment Kelsey was born, Catherine had known something wasn't right. Clear thinking, along with her determination to find the best medical care, had brought them this far. And clear thinking would help her find the cure for her daughter. No frazzled, armchair quarterback could tell her what was best for her baby. She'd think of something. She always did.

Catherine took a deep breath and removed the biggest prescription bottle from the baggie. She shook it well then filled the oral syringe. Lifting Kelsey from the stroller, she worked to rouse her. "Here you go, punkin." She gently pinched Kelsey's cheeks into the formation her stepson Jonathan called "the guppy" and shot the contents into her daughter's mouth.

Holding Kelsey tight, Catherine waited for the retching. She felt the ragged expansion of her daughter's ribcage, bones so fragile they could be easily crushed under her grip. Tears, hot and angry, stung Catherine's eyes. She buried her face in Kelsey's hair, hiding her fear from Susan.

How much time? Did this question haunt every mother? If it didn't, it should. No one was promised more than the present moment, and if Dr. Finke didn't have good news, there would be no future.

She refused to dwell on the possibility. The ventricular septal patch was holding. If she didn't cling to the hope that this advanced prosthetic mesh would keep the hole in Kelsey's heart sealed, her own heart would fail.

Want to continue reading?
Grab your copy today HERE!

PORT OF ORIGIN: BOOK TWO

PORT OF ORIGIN is the story of how far two fathers will go to save their children during a global pandemic. Don't miss this high-octane medical thriller. Grab your copy HERE today.

PROLOGUE

PORT OF ORIGIN

Off the coast of Cameroon, Central Africa

Since ancient times, the sea had been generous. Tuna. Sardines. Ocean prawns big as a man's hand. But those days of plenty had vanished in the wake of the foreign trawlers whose illegal fishing practices were destroying the coastline's natural resources. Dabir watched the moon slip behind a veil of clouds, leaving him and his brothers to navigate the vast Atlantic in an eerie shroud of darkness. From his position at the end of the boat, he could see little beyond the shadowy silhouettes of his father and his two younger brothers.

He stopped rowing for a moment as he waited for the sharp tug of the nylon fishing net that would signal the night's first catch. A wave smashed against the side of the narrow craft, reminding him of the dangers of straying too far into the open waters. He searched for the light of the trawlers that swept the sea's floor with their ghostlike underwater lights while their wide metal jaws devoured everything in sight, but tonight there was no sign of the floodlights used to lure the fish into their nets. Which meant the deadly boats could be anywhere, trying to avoid the overworked coastal patrols searching in vain for those illegal vessels that strayed into the zone reserved for the smaller vessels. All

Dabir could do was pray his father's boat steered clear of the stealthy trawlers that prowled the darkness. And pray that they would catch enough fish to feed their family another day.

Except for the rhythmic slap of waves against the boat and the distant roar of the incoming tide against the shoreline, a silence settled between them. His brothers, Leiyo and Chomba, were too young to recall the sea's bounty or the fat prawns found where the river emptied into the ocean. Even he barely remembered the feel of a full belly and a nice profit. But so far their efforts, like the night before, and the one before that, had brought nothing but a meager catch of tiny fingerlings. No fish meant famine, which was why he'd left university in the capital in order to help provide for his family. And to ensure his son didn't have to do the same thing.

Anger rose, breaking the surface like the great blue marlin, but resentment would do nothing to fill the stomachs of his brothers or his wife and young son. Ignoring the gnawing emptiness in his gut, he waited for the dawn that would soon arrive, bringing with it the fiery ball that splashed pink across the distant horizon.

His wife would be among the women who lined the shoreline with their empty metal pans on their heads anticipating the dozens of small wooden canoes, with their colorful painted sides, to return with a better catch than the night before. Once again, he would disappoint her.

"We need to change our course," Dabir's father shouted and dug his paddle hard into the choppy water.

A spray of saltwater brushed his face, burning Dabir's chapped lips. He searched for the horizon as he rowed, but the black night made it impossible to see.

And his empty stomach made it impossible to go home too soon.

Dabir heard the low rumble of the trawler before he saw it.

A sliver of moonlight broke through the clouds and settled on the side of the rusty hull of the giant trawler that dwarfed their wooden pirogue. The small boat tipped in the wake of the larger vessel.

"Hold on," Dabir screamed.

Their wooden boat groaned then split in two. The smashed skiff plunged into the murky waters, sucking Dabir into its depths.

He gasped for air as the sea engulfed him. Panic flooded his chest.

Disoriented, he searched for the surface, but only darkness surrounded him. Lungs threatened to burst. A trail of moonlight glistened above him, revealing a stream of tiny bubbles. He propelled himself upward, emerged, then filled his lungs with air.

Something thrashed in the water a boat length away.

Dabir grabbed a splintered piece of wood and bridged the distance between them. Leiyo and Chomba struggled to stay afloat on a jagged piece of wreckage.

"Where's Father?" Leiyo shouted.

"Don't let go," Dabir shouted back. "I'll find him."

Senses heightened, Dabir searched the dark, bobbing surface of the endless Gulf of Guinea for a sign of their father. His muscles cramped. Every second that passed pushed him and his brothers closer to succumbing to the deadly currents. But he would not return to his family's compound without his father.

He screamed his father's name over and over again. Silence greeted him. Something brushed across his arm and Dabir felt his heart plummet. The still body of his father floated to the surface. He reached out to grasp his cold hand as the trawler veered away from them, its foreign captain unaware of the fractured wreck beneath his ship's massive hull.

Dabir pulled the limp body against him and swore his revenge. They'd taken his livelihood, and now his father. The men in those giant ships would take nothing more.

CHAPTER ONE

PORT OF ORIGIN

Southern California

Consider the problem. Execute the moves. Summit.

Josiah Allen mentally repeated his life's mantra as he hung from the hairline crack snaking up a crag of El Capitan. A chilly Pacific wind sanded his knuckles and his fingertips were blistered, but he'd never let pain slow him down. Getting to the top despite the obstacles was something he'd learned how to do a long time ago. Willpower had made him one of the best plastic surgeons in the country. Today, he intended to reach another one of his goals: climbing one of the toughest monoliths in the world.

He strained against the taut belay rope connecting him to his wife perched on a narrow ledge fifteen feet below.

"Slack, Camilla." Arms and legs burning from the lactic acid building up in his tense muscles, his feet scrambled to find a toehold. "Camilla?" His desperation bounced off the three-thousand-foot rock tower and came back to him silent.

Josiah risked a swift glance over his shoulder. Camilla, beautiful in her form-fitting spandex and helmet, studied him with an impish grin.

"Today, Monkey Shine," he shouted over the wind.

She shook her head and her black braid wrapped around the slender neck he loved to kiss. "I'm not letting you go any higher, *Dr. Allen*, until I'm sure you're as proficient with all of those shiny new cams racked on your harness as you are with a scalpel." Her brows lifted in a doubtful arch.

"Very funny, *Dr. Allen*."

Neither ever let the other off the hook when it came to their competitive nature. In fact, it was Camilla's drive and brilliance in the cadaver lab that had drawn him to the Venezuelan beauty their first year of medical school. Together, they'd climbed to the top of their chosen fields of practice. He, for one, was looking forward to their sharing the view from the top for many years to come. Summiting El Cap was only one mountain on his list of accomplishments he'd yet to achieve.

Josiah shifted his weight to his left hand and removed a medium-sized cam from his gear strap with his right. "When have I ever steered you wrong, my love?"

"Castle Rock." Her reply bounced off the granite.

He slotted the head of the cam into an overhead fissure. "That was a freak rainstorm."

"In Seattle?"

"Okay, so it ruined your hair." He pulled the trigger on the cam. The reassuring ping reverberating in the canyon told them both he'd chosen the perfect tool. In the ten years they'd been climbing together, he'd made plenty of mistakes. Camilla didn't need any more ammo to twist his impetuous nature into a noose around his neck, but he could tell from the way her dark brown eyes twinkled he'd just tossed her a rope. "That all you've got, woman?"

"Flatiron." Her grin was smug, her confidence as sexy as her long, shapely legs.

"Freak snow."

She jammed her rope-wrapped fist into one of the curves right above those perfect hips. "Colorado? In November?" Her laughter, like hot chocolate in front of a crackling fire on a snowy night warmed him to the core. Perfection with whipped cream. His Camilla.

Josiah jiggled the cam to make sure all four friction lobes had caught. "Early November. Really more late-ish October." He stretched his rope to clip into the carabiner hanging from the cam. Three inches short. He was stuck until she cut him some slack. "Your point?"

"What if I'm tired of getting wet?"

"Come on, admit it, Dr. Allen"—he cast his best provocative wink to egg her on—"you love it when I warm you up."

Her cheeks flushed the pink-grapefruit of a California sunset. "Dr. Allen." She placed a long slender finger to her lips, the same one that could slip inside a child's heart and fix a broken valve with lightning speed. "The neighbors." She jutted her perfect chin at the climbing party seventy-five feet above them. "Newbies," she mouthed.

He glanced at the two-man team huffing and hoisting a hundred-pound haul bag full of supplies. Loud, cocky, and loaded with more gear than ten people would need for a five-day climb, these newbies had been an irritant all day. He hated the snarled traffic jams inexperienced climbers and good weather invariably caused on the wall.

"Maybe it's time we bought our own slab. One so remote, I wouldn't have to share you with anyone but God."

"What's your hurry, big boy?" She tugged on the rope and it pulled his waist toward hers. "We've got the next five days."

"You know that by day three you'll be begging me to go home."

"I trust your sister with our little girl. Rachel will spoil Emma rotten."

"Plus, she'll have obliterated every germ from our house."

"I like having an infectious disease specialist in the family. I'll miss her when she goes to Africa."

"Hey, I said we'd go. . .someday," he said.

"Consider the problem. Execute the moves. Summit." His wife threw his own mantra back at him with a tone of challenge he found hard to resist.

"For you, I'd even get on a boat."

"That's a pretty serious promise for someone who's afraid of water," she teased.

"I'm not afraid. I just prefer clear heights to murky depths."

Camilla lifted her chin and dragged her hand seductively down her torso. "Then let's just sit back and enjoy the view, shall we Dr. Allen?"

"Woman, you're a view I could look at all day—"

Snap.

"Rock!" Freaked-out shouts from above jerked Josiah's head up.

An overloaded haul bag plummeted toward him.

"Camilla!" Josiah flung himself out of the way just before the duffel whizzed past him. The force spun him around and slammed his shoulder against the cliff face. He grabbed the rope that connected him to his wife and pulled back a limp, severed thread.

"Camilla!"

Josiah's frantic gaze careened off the ledge at the exact same moment a woman's body, the body he knew better than his own, catapulted through the void.

"Camilla!" His raw scream followed her twisty-turns and slow-motion somersaults. His hands clawed at the empty air.

One second, she was there. The next. . . "No! God! No!"

"Daddy?" A small hand shook his shoulder. "Daddy!"

Josiah sat straight up. His eyes flew open. Sweat dripped from his forehead. Expensive bedside tables and lamp-like shapes swirled in a gray fog that smelled of burnt toast. Head pounding and heart ricocheting against his chest, he tried to make out how he'd descended a mountain and ended up in their master bedroom.

Breath ragged, he squeezed his eyes shut. In a desperate attempt to remove the weight obstructing his air supply, he dragged his hands across his face. Stubble pricked the smooth palms that reeked of sweat and surgical latex.

Something poked at his leg. "Daddy?"

He dug at his sunken eye sockets, but no amount of rubbing could get at the jackhammer throb. He forced his eyes to open, cringing at the light shards piercing his corneas. He let his hand wander to *her* side of the bed. Empty and cold.

"Daddy, phone."

Slowly, his sleep-deprived vision cleared. "Emma?" The croaky and foreign voice surely didn't belong to him.

His daughter, dressed in a Barbie nightgown and a shiny plastic tiara, clutched his expensive new cell phone in one hand, a banana in the other. Her flawless face was a mini version of Camilla's—except for her eyes. Ocean-blue and narrowed with concern, they had him pegged for the loser he'd become.

He ran his tongue around the inside of his dry mouth, trying to work up enough saliva to speak. "Who is it, Cricket?"

"Aunt Rachel." Emma held out the phone. "She wants to talk to you."

He swallowed the chalky and bitter spit he'd mustered. "Can I call her back?"

"No. She says it's important." She prodded his leg with the banana. "Are you awake, Daddy?"

"I am now." Josiah tried to swing his feet to the floor, but the sweat-drenched top sheet had bound his scrub-clad legs in a twisted vine. He remembered eating a bowl of cereal when he dragged through the door around three am. He did not remember falling into bed in the same clothes he'd worn for ten hours in the OR.

"Give me a minute." He fought the bedding like the reoccurring nightmare that would not let him go.

His daughter put the phone to her ear. "Aunt Ray, Daddy has to potty, then he can talk."

"Em!"

Her face sobered and he immediately regretted raising his voice. "Sorry, Cricket." He patted the bed. "You know how I am before I have coffee."

She nodded. "Worse than a bear in spring."

Camilla's old sayings coming out of Emma's young mouth punched him in the gut every time. "You gonna share that banana?"

Emma eagerly broke the fruit in half. "I made toast, too." She used her half of the banana to point out the tray at the foot of his bed.

"Emma Grace." He crammed banana into his mouth. "We've talked about needing a grown-up present before you use electrical appliances."

"You also told me civilized people never talk with their mouths full." She scrambled up beside him, dragging the bruised fruit with her. She held out the phone. "You ready to talk?"

He shook his head.

Emma regarded him for a brief instant then raised the phone to her ear again. "Aunt Ray, I have a loose tooth."

Josiah couldn't believe he'd allowed himself to sink to such a pitiful state that he'd rather let a child cover for him than explain his decision to his sister.

He snagged a piece of toast from a princess plate. He could hear Rachel gushing on about what a big girl Emma was and promising her she would send the tooth fairy a notification email the moment it fell out.

Then he heard, "Let me talk to your father." Rachel's tone, no longer gushy had become all lab-geek serious.

He was in for the tongue-lashing his late-night text deserved. A real man would have called his only sister to explain his decision. Rachel's sacrifice of leaving her beloved medical ship for over a year in order to devote her attention to him and Emma had earned her that much consideration and much more after. . .He still couldn't say the words. *Camilla died.*

"Put him on now, Em!" Rachel's voice had risen to the same level he'd once heard her use on some CDC Director after he failed to take her advice on an outbreak that had hit and killed kids in several states.

Emma lowered the phone. Her gaze locked with his. She shrugged and held out the phone. "I tried, Daddy."

If he could take back the last twenty months and restore his little girl's innocence, he'd cut off his operating hand.

Steeling himself, he dropped his half-eaten piece of toast on the princess plate and took the call. He motioned for Emma to go on about her business. She acted like she didn't see the gesture and wiggled deeper into the pillows piled on Camilla's side of the bed. Since his wife's death, Emma had become more like his clone than his child. He watched her slender fingers set to work peeling back the banana's yellow skin, the precise movements of a skilled surgeon.

Thanks to Camilla, fixing what was wrong was in Emma's genes. Not a single detail would ever get past this inquisitive little stalker.

Josiah kissed the crooked part on the top of Emma's head, careful to avoid the bejeweled crown that Camilla had given her before...she died.

The sweet smell of tear-free shampoo brought a lump to his throat. Camilla had insisted her baby would have very few reasons to cry.

He put his feet on the floor and raised the phone to his ear. "Hey, Ray."

"A text, Joey? Really?" Rachel growled. "When did you become such a coward?"

Josiah dragged his palm over the two-day stubble on his face. "Top of the morning to you, too, sis."

"I'm not going to take no for an answer," she shrilled. "This is your chance to do what Camilla always wanted the two of you to do together."

At the scorching reminder, he yanked the phone from his ear, counted to five, and went in to settle this thing. "I'm not following you out to sea."

"The *Liberty* ports in one place for months at a time."

"What about Emma?" he asked. "Think my six-year-old will be okay if I just leave her home with the keys to the Porsche and a no-limit credit card?"

"Lots of our docs bring their families."

"I'm not taking my daughter to Africa, Ray."

"You don't get to bail on life on my watch, brother."

"This isn't your watch. It's mine now." From the silence, his words had cut like a scalpel.

"I love you, Joey. But you've left me no choice. I have to consider the welfare of my niece above your need to hole up in an operating room."

He recoiled at the viper-strike accuracy of her diagnosis. The little sister who used to believe he walked on water knew he was sinking. Her disappointment was another stone crushing his chest.

A lonely burn radiated through him. "My work is no less important than yours."

"Emma still has one parent and she deserves to have him present in her life."

"Daddy?"

Josiah froze. He'd forgotten Emma was sitting right there, listening to every word. Again. Rachel was right, he wasn't fit to be a single parent.

He turned. "Cricket, I…"

She held out a jagged chunk of banana. "I saved you the biggest piece."

Guilty bricks were stacked so high on his shoulders he could barely lift his arm to take the banana. "Thanks, Cricket." He cleared his throat and returned to his phone conversation. "I'm sorry, Ray. That was out of line."

He heard Rachel release a pained sigh. "I know you think you won't be able to guarantee Emma's safety on some rusty bucket of bolts in a third-world country, but the *Liberty* is a first-rate, state-of-the-art American medical facility. We have a school, full-time childcare, and a movie theater. It's a floating suburb, complete with kids Emma's own age. Having someone besides her old man to talk to couldn't possibly put her at risk."

"What about exposing her to who-knows-what?" Fear tinged his voice. "You may be God's gift to infectious diseases, but there's stuff over there no one's seen, let alone developed a cure for."

"You know Camilla always wanted to do this."

"Camilla also wanted to climb Everest."

"Camilla loved adventure as much as we do," Rachel reminded him. "If she had this opportunity, what do you think she would do?"

Josiah pinched the bridge of his nose, but the guilt pulsed through his veins afresh. How many times had he second-guessed his decision to take Camilla climbing?

"We couldn't have stopped her," he mumbled.

"When Camilla set her mind to something…" Rachel paused. "She wasn't afraid of dying and she lived right up until she took her last breath. Your wife wouldn't stand for the way you've backed away from life and you know it, Joey."

"What about my practice?"

"Sell it. Plenty of greedy chumps out there are anxious to plump the wrinkles of the rich and famous."

"What about when I come back?"

"Start over. Maybe even open that free clinic Camilla always wanted."

"I can't."

"Take a leave of absence if you don't want to sell to your partners," Rachel said. "Heaven knows you haven't allowed yourself a day off since the funeral."

"No."

"I know how you feel, Joey."

"No offense little sister, but being stood up at the alter isn't quite the same as losing the mother of your child." He knew he couldn't have hurt her more if he'd taken his scalpel and cut her open. She'd struggled since Aiden Ballenger's betrayal, but she hadn't squirreled herself away in her lab. He hated how the inability to move on tasted in his mouth. "Ray, I'm —"

"At least say you'll think about it."

He couldn't stand the ache of loss that resonated in her voice. "Ray, I appreciate everything you've done for us. Really, I do. But Emma and I have to figure this out on our own now."

"Can you at least do one thing for me?"

"Sure."

"Ask Emma what *she* wants to do."

"She's six."

"Going on thirty," Rachel said. "You know she's been listening this whole time. Ask her."

Josiah sighed and looked at Emma. This little girl was all he had left of Camilla. And when she stared at him with Camilla's same expectant expression, his guilt became unbearable.

"You don't want to go Africa, do you, Cricket?"

Emma threw her arms around his neck and wrapped her lanky little legs around his waist. "I do, Daddy!" In her hopeful gaze, it was as if every promise he'd ever made to Camilla waited to be fulfilled.

Against his better judgment, he swallowed his hesitation. "Africa it is." On the other end of the phone, Josiah could hear his sister cheering. "Two weeks, Ray. That's all I can give you."

"Only two weeks?"

He peeled his daughter off him and sat her on the bed. "Take it or leave it."

Rachel didn't hesitate. "I'll take it."

"You better pray I don't regret this, sister."

"Come to Africa, and I'll help you burn that ugly pile of regret you carry around, brother."

"On the water?" he scoffed. "Won't be much of a fire."

Want to continue reading?
Grab your copy today here!

ALSO BY LISA HARRIS

AGENTS OF MERCY THRILLERS

Ghost Heart

Port of Origin

Lethal Outbreak

Death Triangle

SOUTHERN CRIMES

Dangerous Passage

Fatal Exchange

Hidden Agenda

THE NIKKI BOYD FILES

Vendetta

Missing

Pursued

A NIKKI BOYD NOVEL

Vanishing Point

STAND ALONE NOVELS

A Secret to Die For

Deadly Intentions

The Traitor's Pawn

MISSION HOPE

Blood Ransom

Blood Covenant

LOVE INSPIRED SUSPENSE

Deadly Safari

Desperate Escape

Taken

Stolen Identity

Desert Secrets

Fatal Cover-Up

Deadly Exchange

No Place to Hide

The O'Callaghan Brothers

Sheltered by the Solider (Book one)

Christmas Witness Pursuit (Book two)

Hostage Rescue (Book three)

Book four coming December 2020

US MARSHAL SERIES

The Escape (November 2020)

The Chase (2021)

HISTORICAL

An Ocean Away

Sweet Revenge

Sign up for Lisa's newsletter and keep up with her latest news and book releases!

ALSO BY LYNNE GENTRY

THE CARTHAGE CHRONICLES

A Perfect Fit (eShort Prequel)

Healer of Carthage

Shades of Surrender (eShort Prequel)

Return to Exile

Valley of Decision

MT. HOPE SOUTHERN ADVENTURES

Walking Shoes

Shoes to Fill

Dancing Shoes

Baby Shoes

WOMEN OF FOSSIL RIDGE

Flying Fossils

Finally Free

First Frost

AGENTS OF MERCY THRILLERS

Ghost Heart

Port of Origin

Lethal Outbreak

Death Triangle

**Sign up for Lynne's newsletters and
keep up with her latest news and book releases!**

NIKKI BOYD FILES

BY LISA HARRIS

A case that has haunted the public and law enforcement for over a decade. Read the stunning conclusion to the Nikki Boyd Files.

MT. HOPE SOUTHERN ADVENTURE SERIES

LYNNE GENTRY

US MARSHAL SERIES

FROM LISA HARRIS

A deperate murderer and a downed plane turn a routine prisoner transfer into a hunt through the rugged pacific northwest.

"Wow! Wow! Wow! This one is a must read. Lisa Harris has done it again."
~A Brooke and her Books

A brand new US Marshal series coming November 2020

WOMEN OF FOSSIL RIDGE

BY LYNNE GENTRY